FROM THE NANCY DREW FILES

THE CASE: Nancy explores the dark side of the human mind as she attempts to draw a psychological profile of a murderer.

CONTACT: Ned's frat brother Parker Wright is counting on Nancy to clear the fog of suspicion hanging over his head.

SUSPECTS: Diana DeMarco—another participant in the research project, she was involved in a secret romance with Wayne.

Larry Boyd—an entrepreneur interested not only in marketing the experiment but in hiding his past . . . a conviction for manslaughter.

Professor Aaron Edberg—he's running the experiment and running the show . . . and no one's going to stand in the way of his success.

COMPLICATIONS: The murder weapon belonged to Parker's father . . . Parker's fingerprints were found on the gun . . . he was alone in the room with the victim when the shots were fired . . . and Nancy's his only hope!

Books in The Nancy Drew Files® Series

#1	SECRETS CAN KILL	#40	SHADOW OF A DOUBT
#2	DEADLY INTENT	#41	SOMETHING TO HIDE
#3	MURDER ON ICE	#42	THE WRONG CHEMISTRY
#4	SMILE AND SAY MURDER	#43	FALSE IMPRESSIONS
#5	HIT AND RUN HOLIDAY	#44	SCENT OF DANGER
#6	WHITE WATER TERROR	#45	OUT OF BOUNDS
#7	DEADLY DOUBLES	#46	WIN, PLACE OR DIE
#8	TWO POINTS TO MURDER	#47	FLIRTING WITH DANGER
#9	FALSE MOVES	#48	A DATE WITH DECEPTION
#10	BURIED SECRETS	#49	PORTRAIT IN CRIME
#11	HEART OF DANGER	#50	DEEP SECRETS
#12	FATAL RANSOM	#51	A MODEL CRIME
#13	WINGS OF FEAR	#52	DANGER FOR HIRE
#14	THIS SIDE OF EVIL	#53	TRAIL OF LIES
#15	TRIAL BY FIRE	#54	COLD AS ICE
#16	NEVER SAY DIE	#55	DON'T LOOK TWICE
#17	STAY TUNED FOR DANGER	#56	MAKE NO MISTAKE
#18	CIRCLE OF EVIL	#57	INTO THIN AIR
#19	SISTERS IN CRIME	#58	HOT PURSUIT
#20	VERY DEADLY YOURS	#59	HIGH RISK
#21	RECIPE FOR MURDER	#60	POISON PEN
#22	FATAL ATTRACTION	#61	SWEET REVENGE
#23	SINISTER PARADISE	#62	EASY MARKS
#24	TILL DEATH DO US PART	#63	MIXED SIGNALS
#25	RICH AND DANGEROUS	#64	THE WRONG TRACK
#26	PLAYING WITH FIRE	#65	FINAL NOTES
#27	MOST LIKELY TO DIE	#66	TALL, DARK AND DEADLY
#28	THE BLACK WIDOW	#67	NOBODY'S BUSINESS
#29	PURE POISON	#68	CROSSCURRENTS
#30	DEATH BY DESIGN	#69	RUNNING SCARED
#31	TROUBLE IN TAHITI	#70	CUTTING EDGE
#32	HIGH MARKS FOR MALICE	#71	HOT TRACKS
#33	DANGER IN DISGUISE	#72	SWISS SECRETS
#34	VANISHING ACT	#73	RENDEZVOUS IN ROME
#35	BAD MEDICINE	#74	GREEK ODYSSEY
#36	OVER THE EDGE	#75	A TALENT FOR MURDER
#37	LAST DANCE	#76	THE PERFECT PLOT
#38	THE FINAL SCENE	#77	DANGER ON PARADE
#39	THE SUSPECT NEXT DOOR	#78	UPDATE ON CRIME
		#79	NO LAUGHING MATTER
		#80	POWER OF SUGGESTION

Available from ARCHWAY Paperbacks

The Nancy Drew Files

Case 80
Power of Suggestion
Carolyn Keene

AN ARCHWAY PAPERBACK
Published by POCKET BOOKS
New York   London   Toronto   Sydney   Tokyo   Singapore

AN ARCHWAY PAPERBACK *Original*

An Archway Paperback published by
POCKET BOOKS, a division of Simon & Schuster Inc.
1230 Avenue of the Americas, New York, NY 10020

ISBN: 0-671-73084-3

First Archway Paperback printing February 1993

10 9 8 7 6 5 4 3 2 1

Cover art by Tricia Zimic

Printed in the U.S.A.

IL 6+

Power of Suggestion

Chapter

One

$\mathbf{B}$ESS, WAKE UP, we're here," Nancy Drew said to her friend Bess Marvin, who was snoring softly in the passenger seat of Nancy's blue Mustang.

"Hmm?" Bess opened her eyes and yawned. "Just when my dream was getting good." She brushed back a few strands of long blond hair that had fallen over her face. "Johnny Lightning was about to ask me to be a backup singer in the Stormkings."

Nancy poked Bess in the ribs with her elbow. "Too bad your dreams are the only place something like that could happen," she teased. "Come on. Ned's waiting for us."

Looking through her windshield, Nancy saw her longtime boyfriend, Ned Nickerson, coming down the snow-covered steps of his fraternity,

Omega Chi Epsilon. Just looking at his tall, athletic frame, wavy dark hair, and warm brown eyes made her smile.

"Hey, check out that cute guy with him!" Bess said, straightening in the passenger seat.

Nancy glanced at the shorter, red-haired guy who emerged from the fraternity behind Ned. "He must be the friend Ned mentioned. Ned said he was sure you two would hit it off," she added, grinning at her friend.

Before she could get out of the car, Ned was knocking on her window. She rolled it down, and he gave her a kiss. She felt a warm tingle pass through her from head to toe.

"Hey, beautiful," he said in a husky voice. "It's about time—I've been watching for your car from the window. I'm glad you could make it up for the weekend. Saturday's party will be the best ever!" He smiled over at Bess. "Hiya, Bess. Where's George?"

George Fayne was Bess's cousin and the third member of the girls' almost inseparable trio. "She couldn't get away," Bess explained. "The girls' volleyball team she coaches has a big tournament tomorrow and Saturday."

She and Nancy climbed out of the Mustang. Nancy pulled her down jacket around her as she was greeted by a blast of cold late afternoon air. She pulled her blue angora hat lower over her reddish blond hair, then threw her arms around Ned and gave him a big hug.

"I see you missed me," Ned said, laughing.

2

"Don't flatter yourself, Nickerson," she teased. "I'm just trying to stay warm!"

Bess smiled over at Ned's friend and held out her hand. "I'd better introduce myself, since Ned's so excited to see Nancy that he's forgotten his manners—I'm Bess Marvin."

"Sorry," Ned apologized, pulling away from Nancy. "Bess, Nancy, this is Parker Wright. He's a new fraternity brother, not to mention Emerson's top gymnast."

"Ned's told me a lot about you," Parker said, flashing Bess a grin as he shook her hand. Although he was only about Nancy's height, five-foot-seven, he was lean and well-built, with green eyes, a shock of auburn hair, and freckles. He wore boots, jeans, and a leather bomber jacket.

"Come on, let's get you two girls settled in at Packard Hall," Ned said. "Parker knows two roommates who are going to be away for the weekend. They said you could stay in their room."

The four climbed into Nancy's Mustang, then drove through the scenic, snow-covered campus. Soon they were at Packard, a brick and steel dormitory that Nancy remembered from her last visit to the college. She parked her car behind the dorm, and the boys helped Bess and her with their luggage.

"Gee, Bess," Parker said as he lifted two huge suitcases from Nancy's trunk, "I guess you're planning to stay here the rest of the semester."

Bess didn't miss his teasing smile. "I never

3

know what I'll need, so I just bring everything," she answered, smiling back.

As Bess bounded up the stairs to open the door for Parker, Nancy noted how he admired her small, curvy figure. She could already feel sparks flying between the two.

The boys led her and Bess to a room on the second floor. It was small, with two beds, two chests, and two wooden desks and chairs. Dark wood paneling covered the walls halfway up, and the rest was painted a warm peach shade. The large window overlooked a snow-covered quadrangle surrounded by campus buildings.

After depositing their bags on the floor, Nancy turned to Ned with a challenging smile. "The party's not until Saturday, right?" she asked. "It's only Thursday afternoon. So what do you have planned for us, Nickerson?"

"Why don't we head over to the student union and decide what to do over some hot cocoa," Parker suggested.

"Great idea," Bess agreed. "There's always something going on there, anyway."

In a few minutes the four teens were outside again. The snow fell gently but steadily as evening approached. The wind had let up, and the fresh snowfall made the whole campus sparkle.

As the four of them walked through the snow, Bess turned to the others and said, "You guys aren't in a hurry to get to the student union, are you?"

Parker shrugged. "I guess not. Why, what did you have in mind?"

"Oh, I don't know," Bess said, smiling mischievously. She ran a few steps ahead, then bent quickly and scooped up a handful of snow. "Maybe something like"—she hurled her snowball, hitting Parker squarely in the chest—"a snowball fight!"

The next thing Nancy knew, they were all laughing and hurling snowballs at one another on the main lawn of the campus.

"Oho!" Ned cried, after Nancy surprised him with a particularly wet snowball. "Now you've turned traitor on me!" He took off after her, caught her, and swept her up in his arms.

"Put me down, Ned!" Nancy demanded. As he whirled her around in his arms, she wrapped her arms around his neck, grabbing the hood of his parka to keep from falling.

"Here goes!" Ned shouted. He sent her flying into the snow, but Nancy hung onto his coat, and he fell with her. They landed in a deep drift. Laughing all the more, they struggled up into sitting positions. "Hi, Nan," he said, planting a snowy kiss on her nose. "I missed you!"

"I missed you, too," she replied softly, sinking into his arms for another long kiss.

"I think we've found the perfect targets," a voice said.

Pulling away from Ned, Nancy saw that Bess and Parker were standing over them, smiling down. They were each holding two snowballs. "No!" Nancy cried, but it was too late.

"We're all soaked!" Nancy exclaimed twenty minutes later as she, Ned, Bess, and Parker entered the student union. They brushed the snow from their parkas and jeans before walking through the ornate foyer of the building. Nancy knew from previous visits that this used to be where the college president lived. Beyond the foyer, the downstairs rooms had been opened up into one huge space that was filled with tables, a coffee shop, and comfortably furnished nooks where students could meet and talk.

They found a table near the door. While Ned and Parker went to get cocoa, Nancy leaned toward Bess. "So, was I imagining things, or is there some electricity between you and Parker?"

"Well, I wouldn't start planning my wedding yet. I mean, we just met," Bess said. "But he's really nice. Ned was definitely right about us hitting it off." She shrugged out of her parka and hung it on the back of her chair. "It just feels . . . I don't know, natural to be with him."

Nancy was happy for her friend. Even though Bess dated a lot, Nancy thought that maybe Parker was a boy Bess could really get serious about.

The girls looked up a moment later, as Ned and Parker returned with four steaming mugs of cocoa. "This isn't how I pictured the famous

Nancy Drew, 'the world's greatest detective and the best girlfriend a guy ever had,'" Parker said, gazing at Nancy. He set a mug down in front of Bess, keeping the other for himself.

Nancy laughed at the way Parker imitated Ned's voice. "You said that about me?" she asked her boyfriend, batting her lashes outrageously.

Parker flicked his thumb at Ned. "He hasn't stopped talking about you since you called to say you'd be coming for the weekend."

Holding up his hands in surrender, Ned admitted, "I'm afraid it's all true." Then he punched Parker lightly on the shoulder. "But you're not supposed to blow my cover like that. I thought you were my friend!"

As the four of them continued to joke around, Nancy didn't miss the way Bess and Parker beamed at each other. She had to admit they looked cute together, and they seemed to have the same sense of humor.

"Say, Parker—it's almost five-thirty," Ned said, breaking into Nancy's thoughts. "Weren't you supposed to be at the psych lab by—"

Parker slapped his forehead. "By five o'clock! I totally forgot!"

"Isn't five o'clock kind of late for a class?" Bess asked.

"Actually, it's a study group," Parker told her. "I was supposed to show up at the psychology lab for a session. I'm part of this experiment . . ." He gave a resigned shrug. "Well, it's too late now. Besides, I'm having too much fun. Maybe I'll just blow it off."

Nancy was startled as a hand clamped down on Parker's shoulder, causing some of his cocoa to splash onto the table.

"I don't think that's such a good idea," a deep, gruff voice said behind him.

A tall, darkly handsome young man loomed over Parker. "I've been looking all over campus for you. You're in big trouble, Parker. And this time I'm not going to bail you out!"

Chapter

Two

NANCY SHIVERED at the cold look in the tall man's eyes. Next to her, Parker was staring up at him nervously.

"What's it going to be?" the man demanded.

Parker shrugged his shoulders in resignation. "Let's go, I guess," he said.

Parker's casual attitude seemed to anger the dark-haired man even more. "Do you think you're doing me a favor, Wright? I'm doing *you* the favor! I could just as easily be in the library, doing my own work."

"No, no, that's okay, Wayne," Parker said quickly. "I appreciate your help. Is Dave still there?"

Wayne shook his head. "We finished up early," he answered. "Even Dr. Edberg's gone. It'll just be you and me. Come on—let's get this over with."

Parker rose and zipped up his jacket. "Sorry, guys," he told Ned, Nancy, and Bess. "Duty calls."

As Parker and Wayne started to leave, Ned suggested, "Hey, Parker, why don't we meet you in front of the psych building when you're done? We can all go to dinner together."

"That'd be great!" Parker said, brightening. "Meet me there a little after seven, okay?"

"Sure," Bess said, smiling at Parker.

As Parker and Wayne started toward the foyer, Nancy turned to Ned and asked, "What was all that about? Who was that guy?"

"That's Wayne Perkins," Ned replied. "He's a graduate research assistant in the psych department, and a real hardnose. He works with Professor Aaron Edberg—he's a hotshot in the department. Parker is in an experimental program that they're running. I don't know too much about it."

"Hey, who's that?" Bess asked, staring behind Nancy.

Turning around, Nancy saw that a beautiful, dark-haired girl had intercepted Wayne and Parker at the archway leading to the foyer.

"That's Diana DeMarco," Ned replied, following Nancy's gaze. "She's a transfer junior. She's been here only a semester, but she's already made a big impression on everyone."

"I'll bet," Nancy said, appraising the girl.

There was something almost haughty about the girl's posture and expression. She wore a tight-fitting neon pink and black ski ensemble that showed off every curve of her terrific figure.

Nancy, Ned, and Bess were close enough to hear some of the exchange between Wayne and the girl.

". . . But, Wayne, it's really important—we need to talk," Diana was saying.

"Not now, Diana. I have work to do. Look, call me tonight, okay? Whatever it is, I'm sure it can wait until then," Wayne replied.

"I don't think it *can* wait," Diana said, her voice taking on a frosty edge.

Wayne gave her a dismissive shrug. "That's up to you," he said. "Do what you like." With that, he and Parker walked through the foyer and were gone.

"I don't think I like this Wayne Perkins guy," Bess said, frowning down at her cocoa. "He seems really cold."

"You're not the only one who thinks so," Ned told her. "He has a way of setting people's teeth on edge." His gaze moved back toward Diana, who still stood by the foyer, her hands clenched into fists. After a moment she too stormed out into the night.

Bess stared after the brunette, then turned to Ned and Nancy. "Well, I don't know about you, but I'm not going to let that guy ruin *my* weekend. I'm ready for some fun!"

*   *   *

"Do you think Parker will like me in this?" Bess asked an hour later, smoothing the skirt of her red cowl-necked sweater dress.

Nancy nodded. "I think he'd like you even if you were wearing a burlap bag," she teased. She glanced down at her own outfit, a brown leather skirt, a cable-knit sweater Ned had given her for Christmas, and warm tights.

After leaving the student union, the two girls had gone to the dorm so they could change into dry clothes. Now they were waiting in the living room of the Omega Chi Epsilon fraternity house while Ned changed. There was a roaring fire in the room's stone fireplace, and several of Ned's fraternity brothers stopped by on their way in or out.

Nancy and Bess knew many of the guys from previous visits, and soon there was a small group of boys sitting with them. Two of them, Howie Little and Craig Watson, were starters with Ned on the Emerson basketball team, the Wildcats, and old friends of Nancy and Bess.

Nancy looked up as a small, skinny guy in glasses came by. "Here's one of our newest brothers, Maury Becker." Howie introduced the newcomer to the girls.

Maury shook Nancy's hand, regarding her seriously. "You know, I did a complete workup on you and Ned for my compatibility program," he said. "You're the most compatible couple I've ever found."

Nancy laughed, but gave Maury a puzzled look. "You've never even seen us together. What's this program you're talking about?"

"See, I factor in all the variables that can disrupt a relationship, then I cross-reference them against the stabilizing elements and both people's personality characteristics—"

Craig Watson interrupted the flow of words, saying, "Enough, pal. You're overwhelming the poor girls." Turning back to Nancy and Bess, he explained, "We call him Maury the Hacker, Omega Chi's resident computer genius. He doesn't need to meet you—all he needs is raw data to feed into his computer."

"The numbers never lie," Maury assured them.

Suddenly the front door flew open, and a massive figure burst in. The muscular boy had a blond crew cut and was wearing a half-open Emerson jacket, with no scarf, hat, or gloves.

"Whoo! It's cold out there!" he cried, shivering and rubbing his hands together.

"Maybe if you wore something warmer than your varsity jacket, you wouldn't be complaining, Webb!" Craig retorted, laughing. "Come on over and meet Nickerson's girlfriend. Nancy and Bess, this is Dave Webb, star fullback of the football team."

"Dave wants to look like a tough guy out on campus," Howie Little added. "But then we have to listen to him whine."

Dave grinned sheepishly. "If I'd known we had visitors, I would've acted more macho," he agreed.

Nancy's eyes automatically shifted to the doorway as Ned came into the room. He was wearing a pair of gray corduroy pants and a black V-neck sweater, and Nancy thought he looked incredibly handsome. He walked over, sat on the arm of her chair, and gave her a kiss on the cheek. She could feel herself turning bright red as his brothers broke into applause.

"I just want to remind you all whose girlfriend she is," Ned said, flashing the guys a grin. Turning to Nancy and Bess, he added, "It's almost seven. We've got to meet Parker."

As they rose, Dave Webb turned to Ned. "Did Wayne Perkins ever find him? Parker had the study session after mine. Dr. Edberg really went on the warpath when Parker didn't show up."

"I guess it's all smoothed over," Ned said. "Parker is at the psych lab now."

"He should really stay on top of this stuff," Dave said, shaking his head.

"We should all stay on Parker's case to be more serious about his studies," Ned agreed. "See you guys later."

After saying goodbye, he, Nancy, and Bess bundled up and went back out into the cold night.

"What a great bunch of guys!" Bess said, looking out at the snow-covered buildings and evergreen trees that dotted the campus.

"The best," Ned agreed.

As the three of them crossed the main lawn, the seven o'clock bells chimed from the carillon tower. Groups of students passed by, talking and laughing. The campus was so beautiful that Nancy didn't want to hurry, despite the cold.

"What's on your mind, Bess?" she asked, noticing her friend's preoccupied look.

Bess frowned. "Is Parker really doing that badly in psychology?" she asked Ned. "I mean, it's so hard to believe—he seems really bright."

"He is. That's not the problem," Ned answered. "Sometimes the college whirl can be distracting, especially for freshmen like Parker. He was in training for gymnastics until the season ended, he pledged the frat, and he went to a few too many parties. It's easy to fall behind."

"That sounds kind of irresponsible," Nancy commented.

Ned shrugged. "Parker's a great guy," he said, "but that might be his one real weakness. He's always had things pretty easy. He's good-looking, nice, athletic, and his folks are really wealthy. His dad owns a huge real-estate company outside of Emersonville. Parker just expects everything to be fun, and when it's not he has a hard time concentrating."

"Psych class wasn't fun?" Bess guessed.

Ned shrugged again. "I guess not. But this study group he's in seems to be helping."

"So what do they do in the group?" Nancy asked, kicking at a clump of snow with her boot.

"I'm not too sure," he replied. "I do know that Professor Edberg has the students listen to subliminal tapes that are supposed to teach them how to study more efficiently."

"Subliminal tapes?" Bess crinkled up her nose. "What are those?"

"I'm not real clear on that," Ned told her. "The way I understand it, they're tapes that have a hidden message underneath the music. You listen to the music and your subconscious mind hears the message."

Bess shot Ned a doubtful glance. "And that works?"

"Beats me," he said, laughing. "You'll have to ask Parker about it. There's the psych building up ahead."

He pointed to an ivy-covered stone building a dozen yards in front of them. There were only a few lights on inside, Nancy noticed as they approached. It looked peaceful and inviting.

They had just reached the steps when the air was shattered by a muffled report. Nancy, Ned, and Bess froze in their tracks.

"Was that a gunshot?" Bess asked, her voice a whisper.

Nancy's heart started pounding. "Definitely," she said. "I think it came from inside the psych building!"

She was halfway up the steps when the front door of the psych building flew open, and Parker Wright stumbled out. He tripped as he hit the steps and fell to his hands and knees.

"Parker!" Bess exclaimed, vaulting past Nancy. Nancy and Ned were right behind her. As they helped him to his feet, Nancy realized he was wearing only his jeans and sweater and he was shivering. Peering into his eyes, she saw nothing but a dazed look.

"Parker, what happened?" Nancy asked urgently. "Did you hear that gunshot?"

Parker stared at her blankly. When she repeated the question, he blinked, then shook his head, as if he were trying to gather his wits. "I—I don't know . . . the music stopped . . . he fell down . . ." he finally stammered.

"Who fell, Parker? Was it Wayne?" Nancy asked.

"The song . . . the song is the same . . . always the same," Parker babbled.

Nancy turned to Bess and Ned, who were supporting Parker, their arms around his shoulders. "He's not making any sense," Nancy said. "I can't stop thinking about that gunshot. We've got to find out what's going on!"

"I'll take Parker into the lobby so he can warm up," Bess offered. "But you guys, be careful!"

As Bess slowly led Parker back up the stairs and into the building, Ned and Nancy raced inside. "I'm pretty familiar with the building," Ned told her. "Edberg's lab is this way."

He led Nancy down a deserted hallway, up a flight of stairs, and around a corner. Nancy's eyes searched every inch they passed, but she didn't see anyone else or spot anything that looked suspicious.

"In here!" Ned said, stopping at a doorway at the end of the second-floor hallway. The door was ajar, and he pushed it open with his gloved hand.

Nancy burst into the room right behind him and took in the scene.

It was a small room, not much bigger than a faculty office. The first thing Nancy noticed was a mirror that covered almost an entire wall of the room. There was a door beside it. A comfortable reclining chair sat in the middle of the room, facing the mirror.

"Ned, look!" Nancy gasped, pointing.

There, partially hidden by the recliner, a crumpled form lay in a pool of blood on the carpet. Ned's face went white as he knelt beside the form.

"Is it—" Nancy began.

"Yeah, it's Wayne," Ned responded, panic creeping into his voice. "He's been shot!"

Chapter
Three

Nancy could hardly breathe as she bent down beside Wayne. Pulling off one glove, she felt his neck for a pulse. There was none.

"He's dead," she said, trying to ignore the sick feeling that welled up inside her.

"But who . . . ? How . . . ?" Ned's voice trailed off as he stared down at Wayne's body.

"That's what we'll have to find out," Nancy said grimly. She was already sorting through the situation in her mind, and she didn't like what she was coming up with. If Parker had been alone in the room with Wayne, then he was sure to be the prime suspect in the killing.

"Hey, there's a gun!" Ned's voice broke into her thoughts. Looking to where he was pointing,

19

Nancy saw a revolver lying on the carpet at the foot of the recliner.

"Don't touch it!" she advised him. "In fact, don't touch anything. We don't want to disturb any evidence. Is there a phone around? We should call the police and an ambulance right away."

Ned nodded. "There's a phone booth down the hall."

After he left the room, Nancy turned back to examine the scene of the crime. The small, windowless room wasn't like any laboratory or classroom she'd seen before. It was softly lit by track lights along the ceiling and was painted a comforting shade of pale blue. The plush carpeting was a slightly deeper shade of blue, marred now by the dark stain where Wayne's body lay.

Against one wall was a solid oak library table with several cushioned, armless chairs. The study group probably worked around the table, Nancy guessed. Parker's leather bomber jacket hung over the back of one of the chairs. The center-piece of the room was the luxurious recliner Nancy had noticed when she first entered. A set of stereo headphones was hooked over the back of the chair. Set against a side wall was what looked like a control panel, with an assortment of lights and switches.

Nancy walked over to the recliner and held her ear next to the headphones, but there was no sound coming from them. If something had been playing before the shot was fired, it had been turned off.

Next, she went over to the door next to the mirrored wall. It was slightly ajar, so she pushed it open and stepped in.

She found herself in a very small room that was less than seven feet deep. From here she saw that the mirror was really two-way glass, allowing an observer to watch the person sitting in the recliner while remaining unseen himself. There was a console against the mirrored wall, with two desk chairs. Built into the console were a computer terminal, a pair of cassette decks, and a microphone. Several file cabinets stood against the back wall.

Nancy couldn't help wondering what all this equipment was for. And what, if anything, did it have to do with Wayne Perkins's murder?

Hearing the approach of sirens, she quickly returned to the room with the reclining chair and made certain her brief examination had disturbed nothing. Soon after, Ned came back, accompanied by a woman in an Emerson campus security uniform and a trim, balding man who looked to be in his early thirties.

"An ambulance is on the way," Ned said, hurrying over to Nancy and squeezing her hand. The two of them watched while the security officer and the other man knelt beside the body. The balding man felt Wayne Perkins's wrist and neck, then looked soberly up at Nancy and Ned.

"He's dead, all right," he confirmed. He rose and shook Nancy's hand. "I'm Dr. Paul Cohen, from the campus infirmary," he said. He indicated the security officer. "Gina here spotted me walking across campus on my way home and asked me to come along. Are you all right?" he asked, looking into Nancy's eyes. "Finding a dead body can be very disturbing."

"I'm fine," Nancy assured him. "I've seen this sort of thing before."

Dr. Cohen looked at her with curiosity. "You have?"

"I'm a detective," she explained. "But our friend Parker seemed really dazed. Maybe you could take a look at him."

She and Ned led the doctor out of the lab. The security officer, who was speaking into a walkie-talkie, turned to them. "You kids stay close by," she said. "I'm going to need statements from you."

When Nancy, Ned, and Dr. Cohen got to the entrance hall of the building, Parker and Bess were leaning against a wall. Parker still seemed dazed, but Bess was holding his hand reassuringly. Her parka was draped over his shoulders.

Nancy and Ned drew Bess aside while Dr. Cohen approached Parker. In an undertone, they told Bess about finding Wayne Perkins's body.

"Oh, no!" she gasped. "Poor Parker! No wonder he's so upset—he must have seen something!"

Nancy wasn't sure if that was the real reason

for Parker's confusion. She turned her attention back to Dr. Cohen, who was bending close to Parker.

"Hello, Parker, I'm Dr. Cohen," he said in a calm, reassuring voice. "Do you remember what happened?"

Nancy could see that Parker's pupils were dilated and his gaze unfocused. He looked past the doctor and shook his head in confusion.

Dr. Cohen felt Parker's pulse and looked into his eyes. Then he turned to Nancy, Ned, and Bess.

"Your friend seems to be suffering from a mild case of shock," he told them. "Keep him warm and sitting here. I'll be back in a moment."

Glancing through the heavy wood and glass doors, Nancy saw that another campus security car and two Emersonville police cars had just pulled up, their lights flashing. An ambulance was right behind them. A small crowd was beginning to gather outside, and one of the campus security guards moved to keep the onlookers from entering the building.

As Dr. Cohen went outside, hurrying over to the ambulance, three uniformed police officers burst into the building, accompanied by a rumpled middle-aged man in a trenchcoat who was chewing on the remnants of a foul-smelling cigar. With them was one of the biggest men Nancy had ever seen. He wore a campus security uniform with gold braid on the cap and shoulder.

"That's Captain Marcus Backman, the new

head of campus security," Ned whispered to Nancy as the group hurried past, toward the stairway. "He was the greatest linebacker Emerson ever had!"

The group of officers was followed by a medic team from the ambulance. They also hustled past Nancy and her friends, accompanied by Dr. Cohen. As Parker watched the parade of officials race past, he started looking more and more confused.

"Wh-what's going on?" he finally asked.

Nancy exchanged an uncomfortable look with Ned and Bess. Could he really not know what had happened? Nancy wasn't sure what to tell him. If he was already in shock, telling him about Wayne Perkins's death probably wouldn't help his condition.

Nancy looked up as Dr. Cohen returned. Captain Backman and the man in the trenchcoat were with him.

"I'm Lieutenant Easterling, homicide, Emersonville PD," the man in the trenchcoat said, speaking around his cigar stub. He focused on Nancy and Ned. "Dr. Cohen tells me you two found the body."

"Body?" Parker repeated, suddenly looking scared. "Wh-what body? Is s-someone dead?"

Captain Backman put a hand on Parker's shoulder. "Take it easy, son," he said in a deep voice. "Everything's going to be all right."

Turning back to Nancy and Ned, Lieutenant Easterling repeated, "Now, you two found the body." When they nodded, he asked, "You're both students here?"

"I am—I'm Ned Nickerson. This is my girlfriend, Nancy Drew. And this is Bess Marvin. They're visiting for the weekend."

Captain Backman turned to Nancy, a surprised expression on his face. "You're Nancy Drew?" he asked.

"So, who's Nancy Drew? Someone special?" Easterling asked, chomping on his cigar.

"Miss Drew is a very talented amateur detective." Backman turned back to Nancy. "I reviewed the security department records when I took this job. You've been a great help to the college in the past."

Easterling gave a dismissive wave in Nancy's direction. "Give me a break," he scoffed. "A teenage detective?"

Nancy felt a surge of anger at the man's attitude. She opened her mouth, but Easterling held up his hand.

"Later," he said. "Right now I want to get the details straight. What were you kids doing here?"

Parker had gradually been coming out of his daze, and now he was lucid enough to respond, "They were here to meet me."

"And you are . . . ?" Lieutenant Easterling asked.

"Parker Wright. I'm a student here."

The lieutenant fixed Parker with a stony gaze as he said, "All right. So where were you when the shooting happened?"

25

"I—I was in the lab, I guess," Parker replied. Nancy noticed that the same look of confusion had come over him, as if he wasn't quite sure.

"What do you mean, you guess?" Easterling demanded. "You were there or you weren't! Did you see anything? Who shot this guy—what's his name?" He turned expectantly to Captain Backman.

"Wayne Perkins," the captain supplied.

"That's right—Wayne. So who shot him? Did you do it?"

The bluntness of the question shocked Nancy. If this was the way Easterling conducted an investigation, then she was unimpressed.

"No—of course I didn't kill him," Parker protested, flustered. "At least, I—I don't think I did."

Easterling let out a sigh. "I can see this is going to be a long night," he said. "I want the four of you to come downtown to the station with me. We're going to need to ask you a few questions."

"Why is this taking so long?" Bess asked.

It was after eleven, and she, Ned, and Nancy had all been questioned extensively by the police at the Emersonville police station. Now they were sitting on a wooden bench in the front room of the station, waiting for Parker. Despite the late hour, several officers were busy at desks in the open room.

"They've been questioning Parker for more than three hours now," Ned said, resting his elbows on the knees of his corduroys. "I hope they're not being too hard on him."

Nancy wasn't sure what to say. She couldn't blame the officers for questioning Parker so thoroughly. She didn't want to believe that Parker Wright was capable of murder, but the evidence seemed to point to him.

The three teenagers looked up as Parker emerged from a hallway to the side of the station's front room, accompanied by Lieutenant Easterling and a uniformed police officer. Nancy's heart went out to Parker when she saw his confused, dejected expression.

"Can we all go now?" Bess asked Easterling as he, Parker, and the police officer approached.

Easterling hesitated before answering. "You three are free to go, but your friend Parker is going to stay here with us for a while."

"What do you mean?" Ned demanded, getting to his feet. "What's the problem?"

"Look," said Easterling. "Parker's fingerprints were all over the gun. He had motive, and he had opportunity."

Nancy gripped the edge of the bench. She had a feeling she knew what the lieutenant was going to say next, and it wasn't good news.

"I don't like to have to tell you this," Easterling went on, "but I've arrested Parker Wright for the murder of Wayne Perkins."

Chapter

Four

"BUT THAT'S impossible!" Bess protested. She looked at Parker, then burst into tears.

Nancy didn't even know she'd been holding her breath until she suddenly let it out in a rush. As she wrapped a comforting arm around Bess's shoulders, her eyes strayed to Parker. He stared down at his feet, but Nancy saw the hot red color that had risen to his cheeks.

Ned took a step toward the policeman. "You've got the wrong suspect," he said heatedly.

"That's for a court to decide," Easterling told him.

"Can we at least have a few minutes to speak to Parker?" Ned pressed.

The lieutenant's gaze went from Ned to Nancy

to Bess. "Yeah, but make it short," he finally said.

Ned put his arm around his friend's shoulders and led him to the bench where Nancy and Bess were sitting. "How are you doing, buddy?" Ned asked.

Parker no longer was the same happy-go-lucky guy Nancy and Bess had met just that afternoon. His face looked haggard, and his gaze darted around nervously.

"I—I guess I'm okay," Parker finally answered. "They let me make some calls. I tried to reach my parents, but they're out of town—out of the country, actually. They're in South America, rafting down the Amazon or something like that. I was home just last weekend, but I totally forgot about the trip until our housekeeper reminded me."

"There's no way to reach them?" Nancy asked, studying Parker. He still didn't seem quite right to her. She had seen many crime suspects, and usually they had strong reactions to being accused. But Parker seemed only depressed and puzzled.

Parker shook his head in answer to her question. "Not right away. The housekeeper promised to keep trying. Maybe it's better this way. How can I ask them to bail me out? I feel so ashamed."

"But you haven't done anything," Bess put in emphatically. "This is all a huge misunderstanding!"

"That's right," Ned agreed. "Besides, bail isn't something you need to worry about. You're an Omega Chi brother now."

Parker raised a questioning brow. "How's that going to help me?"

"Hey, maybe bail wasn't on anyone's mind when the Omega Chi emergency fund was started, but I'm sure the brothers will agree that this is a real emergency."

Easterling had been waiting impatiently a few feet away. Now he came over and said, "Sorry, kids. Time's up."

"Lieutenant, can't we bail Parker out tonight?" Ned asked.

The lieutenant shook his head. "You'll have to wait until the arraignment tomorrow morning. I'm afraid Parker's a guest in our motel tonight."

Parker borrowed a pen and a piece of paper from Lieutenant Easterling and wrote down a name, then handed the paper to Ned. "This is my father's attorney. I wasn't able to reach him, either. I left a message on his answering machine, but I'd appreciate it if you'd call him, too."

Ned promised he would. Nancy gave him an encouraging smile, while Bess kissed him on the cheek. "We'll see you in the morning," Bess promised. Then Easterling led Parker down the hall.

A police officer drove Nancy, Ned, and Bess back to the Emerson campus, letting them off at Packard Hall. During the ride, Nancy sat silently, going over Wayne's murder and Parker's arrest in her mind.

"Hey, Nan, you've been very quiet since we left police headquarters," Ned said, pausing outside the dormitory.

Nancy took a deep breath. "I know you both like Parker a lot," she began cautiously, "but so far all the evidence points to him as Wayne's murderer. He was the only one in the lab, his prints are on the gun, and he doesn't have an alibi."

"Then the evidence is wrong!" Bess declared.

"Bess is right," Ned added. "Parker wouldn't hurt a fly."

Nancy hoped her friends were right. But she couldn't rid her mind of the doubts about Parker's innocence.

"I'm so glad Parker is free again!" Bess exclaimed as she, Nancy, and Ned left the Emersonville courthouse at nine the following morning.

"Me, too. I'm sure it meant a lot to him that so many of the brothers showed up," Nancy added, nodding toward the group of guys walking down the courthouse steps in front of them.

Ned nodded proudly. "The guys really wanted to show Parker that we're behind him," he said. "I couldn't believe how much bail the judge ordered, though. It's a good thing Parker's lawyer was able to post bail—the Omega Chi emergency fund wouldn't have been nearly enough."

Nancy saw Parker just ahead of them on the steps. During the arraignment, he'd still seemed a little dazed to her. Now he was talking with his lawyer, a distinguished, gray-haired man named Mr. Caputo.

Looking ahead, Nancy saw a bearded, middle-aged man wearing a tweed hat and an overcoat getting out of a car. When the bearded man saw Parker, he peered at the young man through thick glasses.

"Professor Edberg," Parker said, looking startled. It was the first sign of animation Nancy had seen on his face all morning.

"Parker, how could you!" Professor Edberg shouted. "I knew you and Wayne hated each other, but to kill him in cold blood!"

Parker blanched. "I didn't—" he began to protest, but the professor shoved past him.

"That young man was the most promising researcher I've ever worked with," Edberg went on. "He was worth ten of you! And you snuffed him out without a second thought—"

"Come on now, Professor," Lieutenant Easterling interrupted. He had been walking behind the group but hurried over to Dr. Edberg when he began speaking. He smoothly guided Edberg around Parker, and the two walked toward the courthouse entrance.

Parker recoiled as though he'd been slapped. Immediately Bess, Nancy, Ned, and some of the fraternity brothers gathered around him, but the look of shock remained on his face.

"Let's go back to the house, buddy," Ned said, putting an arm around Parker's shoulders. "After what you've been through, you need some food."

The group waited while Parker spoke briefly to his lawyer. Then Mr. Caputo left, and a small caravan of cars made its way back to Omega Chi Epsilon. Soon Nancy, Bess, Ned, and Parker were sitting at a long table in the fraternity's dining room, eating a breakfast of bagels, rolls, eggs, and bacon.

"Another bagel, Nancy?" Howie Little offered from across the table.

"Thanks, no. I couldn't eat another bite," Nancy told him. "How about you, Bess?"

Bess held up her hand in refusal, her mouth too full to respond.

Since they'd arrived, a constant stream of fraternity brothers had passed through. Some sat down for a full breakfast, while others just raced in, grabbed a bagel or a roll, and dashed off. Everyone had an encouraging word for Parker, Nancy noticed.

After they'd all eaten, Nancy turned to Parker, an inquisitive look on her face.

"Oho, I know that look," Ned spoke up from Nancy's other side. "Detective Drew is about to swing into action!"

"Are you going to help me, Nancy?" Parker asked eagerly. "Can you find out who really killed Wayne?"

Nancy flashed Ned a quick look. She knew he meant well, but she couldn't try to prove Parker

33

innocent when she wasn't certain herself that he *hadn't* murdered Wayne. Better take it slow, she thought.

"I'd like to, Parker," she said carefully. "But first I need more information. "What did Professor Edberg mean about you hating Wayne?"

"He's wrong—I didn't hate Wayne!" Parker burst out. "I respected him. He was trying to help me, I knew that. He just had a way of going about it that drove me crazy." Parker was emphatic, almost wild, and Nancy realized just how tightly wound he was.

"Wayne did that to everyone," Howie added, reaching for another bagel. "I took one of Edberg's classes last year. Wayne was the teaching assistant, and he was really hard on all of us. For a guy studying psychology, he didn't have much in the way of people skills."

Nancy thought back to the rude way Wayne had spoken to Parker. "Still, there seemed to be something special about the way he singled you out, Parker," she persisted.

"Yeah, I guess," Parker said. "He really came down hard on me when I started flunking his quizzes. It all came to a head after he talked to my dad."

"He called your father? Teachers do that in college?" Bess asked, looking surprised.

Parker shook his head. "No—I visited my folks one weekend. A psych quiz fell out of my notebook, and my dad found it. He got real angry at me. Dad called Edberg's office, but he got Wayne on the phone instead."

"Uh-oh. Sounds like trouble," Howie remarked.

"You bet," Parker agreed. "Wayne really gave him an earful. I don't know exactly what he said, but after they spoke, Dad threatened to cut off my allowance and take away my car. Later that night Edberg called. I guess Wayne had spoken to him. He and my dad talked—and that's how I ended up in the study group."

"What happened after that?" Bess asked.

"I confronted Wayne," Parker replied. "I told him he'd gotten me in big trouble, and he called me a lazy, spoiled rich kid. I guess he'd worked all his life. . . ."

As he spoke, Parker twisted his mug of cocoa on the table. "Anyway, I got mad and said some things I shouldn't have. Then he got madder. We were just about to start swinging at each other when Dr. Edberg came in and broke it up."

"You got into a fistfight with a teaching assistant?" Craig Watson asked.

Parker nodded sheepishly. "But we worked it out the next day. I apologized for losing my cool, and he said he was sorry he got me in trouble. Look, we never really liked each other, but he was helping me out, and I sure didn't hate him."

"This isn't good, Parker," Nancy said. "Your argument gives the prosecution a motive. They can say you killed Wayne in a fit of anger. They can say you two fought again, and this time you cracked."

"No way!" Parker protested. "That's not how it happened. I'm sure it's not!"

"If you want me to try to help you, maybe you'd better tell me what *did* happen in the psych lab last night," Nancy said gently.

"But that's just it!" Parker wailed. "I'm sure I didn't kill Wayne—I *know* I didn't—but maybe I did. I don't know!"

Bess, Ned, and the few fraternity brothers who hadn't left yet stared at Parker from around the table. Nancy could see that they were all taken aback by his outburst.

"What do you mean, you don't know?" Nancy asked carefully.

"I mean, I don't know! It's like I told the police, everything from when I left you guys to when you found me outside the psych building is a blank. I feel as if my memory's been erased. I can't remember a thing!"

Chapter

Five

HOW COULD YOU forget everything?" Nancy asked.

She saw that no one was eating any longer. Everyone was staring at Parker. He was becoming more wild-eyed, and he began to perspire. His breath was coming in quick, shallow gasps.

Bess took his hand soothingly. "Hey, Parker, it's okay. Calm down."

"Sometimes a severe shock can have this effect," Nancy explained. "A person sees something he or she can't deal with, so that person experiences amnesia about the incident. My dad once told me about a case he had like that."

Parker's breathing slowed, and he looked at Nancy. "Really?" he asked. "I thought I was the only one. Nothing like this has ever happened to me before." He sat up straighter in his chair. "But I want you to know I could never kill anyone. Never! And I'll help you prove that, any way I can."

Nancy felt a wave of compassion for Parker. "I'll definitely do whatever I can to find out what really happened," she told him.

"That would be great!" Parker said. "Thanks."

"Don't get too excited," Nancy cautioned, holding up a hand. "We don't know where the investigation might lead. But I promise I'll do my best to get at the truth."

Parker grinned at her. "That's all I can ask. Now, how can I help you?"

"I'm afraid you *can't* help, Parker," she replied. "You're the prime suspect in a murder case. The best thing you can do is keep a low profile and stay out of trouble."

She gave him a careful look. "There *is* one thing you can do right now, though," she added.

"Tell me!" Parker said eagerly.

"Go to sleep. You look exhausted."

With a weary nod, Parker said, "I didn't get much sleep at all last night," he admitted. "But if I miss my morning classes . . ."

"We'll cover for you," Ned cut in. "Give me your class schedule. I'll make sure someone takes notes for all your classes."

"You should definitely take it easy today," Bess chimed in. "Tomorrow's Saturday, so you won't have to worry about classes for a few more days."

Parker looked as if he might object, but a yawn swallowed his words. "Okay," he said, giving in. "I guess I do need to sleep."

As he went upstairs, Bess turned to Ned. "Will you make sure he tries to relax today?" she asked.

Ned and the other fraternity brothers promised to keep an eye on Parker for the rest of the weekend.

"I'm so glad you're going to take Parker's case," Bess said to Nancy.

"I don't know what we'll find," Nancy cautioned, "but I do know where to start."

"Where?" Ned wanted to know.

"Upstairs. Dave Webb said last night that he's in Parker's study group. I don't think he's left for class yet—I've been watching for him."

"I'll go get him," Ned said, jumping up and heading for the stairs.

One by one the boys drifted off, leaving Nancy and Bess sitting alone at the dining room table. "Come on, Bess, let's clean up," Nancy suggested. Together they piled up the dishes. They were just about to start carrying them to the kitchen when Ned returned.

"You don't have to do that," he said. "You're our guests."

"The guys will take care of the dishes," Dave Webb agreed. He stood next to Ned. He was wearing jeans, sneakers, and a sweatshirt.

"Maybe you can start by telling us about Dr. Edberg's study group," Nancy suggested as the four of them moved into the living room and settled on the sofas and chairs near the fireplace.

"What do you want to know?" Dave asked.

Nancy paused for a moment, thinking. "Well, how does it work? What do you do in the group?"

"There are six of us—three guys and three girls. We all meet together on Wednesday nights in a regular study session with Dr. Edberg and Wayne."

"To study psychology?" Ned asked.

"Not just that. We each review our notes from other classes for the previous week."

"But last night was Thursday," Bess put in.

Dave nodded, brushing his hand across his blond crew cut. "Yeah—we also have individual sessions. Parker and I come in for an hour each on Thursdays."

"What do you do in those sessions?" Nancy asked. "I saw a chair in the middle of the room."

"Yeah. It's weird but really relaxing. That's the most comfortable chair I've ever sat in. It's got dozens of different positions. I sit in the chair, get comfortable, put on headphones—and listen to music." Dave shrugged. "That's all for the whole hour. Dr. Edberg said that there are subliminal messages on the tapes, telling us how to be better students, but I never heard them."

"That's because you only hear them subconsciously," Nancy said. "Did it help?"

Dave shrugged again. "I guess so. My grades

have started to go up and not just in psych. It's as if I'm listening better in all my classes."

"Couldn't that just be because you're spending extra time studying?" Bess asked.

"Maybe," Dave said. "I guess I never thought of that. Edberg *did* say that some students might get a tape with no subliminal message—so he could measure whether people who heard the message actually did better in school than people who didn't."

Nancy tried to turn the conversation to Wayne's murder. "About last night," she began. "Did you see Parker?"

"No," Dave replied. "He was supposed to come in at the end of my session, but he never showed. Edberg was really ticked off. He wanted to throw Parker out of the group, but Wayne wanted to give him another chance. I said he might be in the student union, since that's where everyone hangs out. So Wayne went to look for him."

"What about Dr. Edberg?" Nancy asked.

"We walked out together," Dave told her. "I think we were the last people in the building. We said good night in the parking lot. Then he got into his car and drove away. I walked around a little, then came back to the house."

So far, Dave wasn't giving Nancy anything new to go on. "Think carefully, Dave. Did you see anyone else at all in or around the building?"

Dave wrinkled his brow and clasped his hands behind his head. Then his eyes lit up. "Come to think of it, there *was* someone. He was going in as we were leaving!"

"Who was it?" Ned asked urgently.

"Just some bald middle-aged guy in an over-coat. I never saw him before—figured he was a professor," Dave answered.

"I'm sure that some of the professors fit that description," Ned said thoughtfully. "Maybe we should look through the faculty photos in a yearbook."

"Dr. Cohen is balding," Bess put in.

"You mean from the infirmary?" Dave asked. "He does the team physicals. It wasn't him."

Bess frowned. "I wonder who it was, then?" she asked. "I mean, if he was still in the building, he could be a witness!"

"Or a killer—don't rule that out," Nancy added grimly. "Dave, keep an eye out for that man, okay?"

Dave promised he would, then got up to go. "I don't want to be late for class," he said. He was heading for the closet when Nancy stopped him.

"Oh, Dave. You said there were three girls in the group."

"Yeah, pretty ones, too," he replied, grinning. "One of them isn't on campus right now—her father died. The other two are roommates, Janis Seymour and Diana DeMarco. They live over in Packard."

"That's where we're staying," Bess said.

"Diana DeMarco," Nancy repeated, searching her memory. "Wasn't she the girl who stopped

Wayne in the student union last night?" she asked Ned.

Ned snapped his fingers. "That's right! She seemed pretty angry with him, too."

"I think we'd better talk to Janis and Diana next," Nancy declared.

"I hope they're here," Bess said later that morning. She and Nancy were standing in the first floor hall of Packard, knocking on the door to Room 106. Ned had gone to class, leaving the two girls to investigate on their own. After walking to the dorm, they had gotten the number of Janis and Diana's room from the directory inside the entrance.

A few moments after Bess knocked, the door opened, and a slim, pretty girl peered out. Although it was late morning, she still wore a bathrobe, and her short black hair was uncombed. She had enormous brown eyes, which were rimmed with red, as though she'd been crying.

The girl sniffled, then asked, "Yes?"

This definitely wasn't the brunette Nancy had seen with Wayne at the student union. "Janis Seymour?" Nancy guessed.

"Yes. And you are . . . ?"

Nancy quickly introduced herself and Bess, then said, "We're friends of Parker Wright. Would you mind if we ask you a few questions?"

"You know Parker?" Janis's brown eyes widened. "Then this must be about Wayne." As she gestured for Nancy and Bess to enter, tears slipped down Janis's cheeks.

Nancy glanced around as she entered the room. The walls were covered with posters, and bottles and tubes were scattered across the dresser tops. There were two desks, both covered with books and papers. A laptop computer sat on one desk, and a small electronic typewriter was on the other.

"Sorry about the mess," Janis said with a wave of her hand. She sat on one of the beds, while Bess pulled up a desk chair and Nancy leaned against a desk.

"I guess you've heard about Wayne Perkins's death," Nancy said, getting down to business.

Janis nodded. "Everyone was talking about it in the hall. I've been a wreck ever since I heard!"

"I guess word travels fast, huh?" Bess said.

"It's a small school—it's hard to keep secrets here," Janis agreed. "I've never seen you two around, though. Are you students here?"

"No, we're just up for the weekend. I'm trying to learn a little about Wayne," Nancy explained.

"Nancy's a detective," Bess explained.

Nancy shot her friend a warning look. She had learned that it was often better not to announce being a detective when she was on a case.

"A detective?" Janis echoed, a doubtful expression on her face. "I don't know what to tell you. They say Parker killed Wayne, but that's impossible, isn't it? I mean, I know they had some arguments, but Parker's so nice."

"What about Wayne?" Nancy asked.

Janis smiled. "He was a really sweet guy. Half the girls on campus had crushes on him."

"Really?" Bess asked, arching a brow. "I thought people didn't like him."

"He acted tough, and he was a hard grader, but that was just because he had high standards," Janis said defensively. "He'd do anything to help if he thought a student was trying. And he was so good looking—but so mysterious!"

"Mysterious?" Nancy asked, her ears perking up.

Janis nodded. "He wouldn't talk about where he came from or about his life before coming here. But he made it sound as if he'd had things tough."

Mmm, thought Nancy, maybe someone from his past had caught up with him. "What about your roommate," Nancy asked. "How well did she know Wayne?"

Janis's friendly attitude suddenly vanished. It was as if a curtain had dropped between her and Nancy. "Diana? You'll have to ask her," Janis said coolly.

Nancy and Bess exchanged a questioning glance. "Do you know where she is?" Bess asked.

"I suppose she's at class. I really couldn't tell you." She eyed them suspiciously. "How do I know you're really a detective? You don't look like one. Maybe you're just a couple of morbid snoops! I think you should leave now."

Nancy could see that it would be useless to

question Janis any further. As Nancy and Bess headed toward the door, Nancy said, "When you see Diana, could you please tell her we'd like to talk to her? We're staying upstairs in Room two-twenty-seven. Or she can call Omega Chi and leave a message for me there."

Janis's only response was a withering look.

"Boy, she sure iced up all of a sudden," Bess said once they'd left the room and were out in the hallway.

Nancy frowned. "That's for sure. It happened as soon as we brought up Diana DeMarco. I wish we could talk to Diana, but since we can't, I'll settle for Professor Edberg. Maybe he can shed more light on Parker's problems with Wayne."

Seeing a pay phone, Nancy used it to call the psychology department for the professor's schedule. "He's getting out of class in about five minutes," she told Bess, hanging up. "Let's go!"

Nancy started for the door, but Bess held her back. "Wait—I just want to call the fraternity to see if Parker's okay." Bess got the number from information, then dialed.

"Can I speak with Parker?" Bess asked. A moment later, Nancy saw her friend's face pale. "What do you mean he's not there? Where did he go?"

"What is it, Bess? What's wrong?" Nancy asked.

In response, Bess handed her the phone. Nancy quickly pressed the receiver to her ear.

"Hello? Bess?"

Nancy recognized Howie Little's deep voice. "Hi, Howie—it's me, Nancy. What's going on?"

"I was telling Bess that Parker's lawyer called with some bad news, and Parker ran out of here."

"What do you mean, bad news? How bad?"

"Real bad. Apparently Edberg said some terrible things about him to the police, but that's not the worst of it. The police traced the gun that killed Wayne," Howie explained. "It was registered to Parker's father!"

Chapter

Six

NANCY COULD HARDLY believe her ears. Her mind was buzzing as she thanked Howie and hung up the phone. The gun was yet another clue that implicated Parker.

"Nancy? What else did Howie say?"

Nancy blinked, then realized that her friend was looking at her expectantly. When Nancy told her about the gun, Bess grabbed Nancy's arm.

"But that still doesn't prove he killed Wayne! I'm sure he's innocent!" Bess protested.

"The gun could have been stolen by someone other than Parker," Nancy said. Still, she had a feeling it wasn't going to be easy to prove that to the police.

"So what do we do now?" Bess asked.

Nancy shrugged. "We keep following whatever leads we get. Let's go talk to Dr. Edberg."

It was a sunny day, but the air was crisp and cold as they walked across campus to the psychology building. Nancy was glad that they'd worn jeans and warm sweaters under their down parkas.

When they reached the three-story stone building, the girls consulted the directory. There were classrooms and labs on the first and second floors, and faculty offices on the third. Nancy and Bess climbed up the stairs to the third floor, arriving at the professor's office just as he was returning from class. Nancy recognized Edberg from having seen him that morning. As he unlocked his office door, she and Bess intercepted him.

"Professor Edberg, may we have a few moments of your time?" Nancy asked.

Edberg turned to her with a smile. "Why certainly," he answered. "I'm sorry, I don't recognize you. Are you in one of my classes?"

Nancy thought quickly. He didn't remember passing them on the courthouse steps that morning. That was good. He might be reluctant to talk with them if he knew the girls were friends of Parker. "No, we're reporters from the student newspaper," she lied.

Edberg scowled. "I'm sorry, young lady, I've already given a statement to the press. Didn't your editor tell you that?"

Nancy didn't miss a beat. "Of course, Professor. But it's not the murder we want to ask you about. The editor-in-chief thought a background piece explaining your work might be helpful. But if it's too much trouble . . ." She gave him a downcast look, then started to turn away.

Edberg's expression immediately softened. "No, no, certainly not. It's always a pleasure to talk about my work. Please, come in."

The walls of his small, comfortable office were lined with bookshelves and filing cabinets. There was barely enough room for the professor's desk and two wooden chairs. As the girls sat in the chairs he explained, "I'm afraid I'm on edge over this horrible business. Wayne Perkins was more than a student to me. He was a protégé—almost a son. I've taken his death quite hard. When I learned that one of my undergraduate students was to blame, well . . ." The professor sighed and leaned back in the desk chair.

Nancy took a pen and notepad out of her purse and began to write. She wanted to make the reporter act convincing. "I understand Parker Wright was in a special study group?" she prodded.

"Yes. He seemed like such a nice kid, although I knew he was troubled. You see, he was under a great deal of pressure from his parents, and he just couldn't meet their expectations. But I never imagined he would crack so violently!

"It's so tragic," the professor went on. "The police do seem certain they have their killer . . .

50

although, of course, the investigation is continuing. I hear they've been interviewing people on campus all morning. I gave my statement earlier —they needed me to identify the body. Terrible . . ."

Edberg had been looking off behind the girls, as though he were thinking out loud rather than addressing them. Now he refocused on Nancy and Bess, saying, "I'm sorry. I said I wouldn't talk about the killing, and here I am doing just that."

If only she could keep him talking about it a little longer, Nancy thought. Then she said, "There's a rumor going around campus. People are saying Parker Wright doesn't remember anything about last night. How is that possible?"

Edberg's attention perked up. "That's a good question, young lady. Actually, that's not an uncommon response," he said, his voice taking on a smooth, professional tone. He took an unlit pipe from his pocket and began to chew on its stem. "You see, his conscious mind can't deal with what he's done, so he's blanked out all memory of the event. No doubt some time soon it will all come pouring back in a devastating rush." He shook his head sadly. "It may well shatter the poor young fellow."

"I understand the study group was using subliminal suggestion tapes," Bess spoke up. "Could that have anything to do with Parker's memory loss?"

"Absolutely not," the professor replied. Then

he wagged a finger at Bess and Nancy. "You're skillful reporters, young ladies. You've cleverly turned me back to your original question. You're interested in my work, right?"

Nancy smiled back at him. "Bess and I want to know about your research and how the study group fit in."

Edberg leaned back in his chair. "The study group is a part of more extensive research, but it's a very important part. You see, my work is based on the principle of subliminal persuasion. I believe that students—indeed, all people— succeed or fail according to their attitudes about themselves and what they are trying to accomplish. A positive attitude brings success; a negative one, failure. These attitudes are deep-seated, existing for the most part in the subconscious mind."

"So that people may not even be aware of them?" Bess put in.

"Exactly," Professor Edberg replied, beaming at her. "My theory—and that of other experimenters, I might add—is that the best way to deal with any negative attitudes is to attack them directly. Go straight to the subconscious, bypassing the conscious mind."

Bess leaned forward in her chair. "That's so fascinating! How do you do it?"

"I was coming to that." Edberg smiled again. "You see, the students in the study group listen to taped music while reclining in a soothing environment. Beneath the sound of the music, so faint they cannot consciously hear them, are recorded messages, telling them how to change their negative attitudes about their ability to perform and how to study using methods that work."

"And that works?" Bess wondered.

"So far we've had very exciting positive results. We've run different study groups every semester for the past two years with remarkable success," Edberg answered.

"Is the school running the project?" Nancy asked, looking up from the notes she'd been jotting down.

The professor took the pipe from his mouth and tapped it on his desk. "Not exactly. The school is very pleased to have me working on this, but funds are tight. I've had to find an outside backer."

"Where does the money come from, if you don't mind my asking?" Nancy asked.

"Of course not." The professor waved away her concern. "It's a matter of public record. As you might suppose, there's a lot of money to be made from selling subliminal tapes, and there are a number of companies around the country doing just that. There are tapes to help people stop smoking, to make them better parents, to teach them geography or learn languages—you name it."

Nancy nodded, encouraging him to continue.

"The potential is really unlimited," the professor went on. "Recently even the federal government has become interested. There are several agencies that would like to use taped study in training programs." He held up a hand. "The government, however, wants scientific proof before it invests in such an approach to teaching. The first company that can offer that proof stands to make a great deal of money on government contracts."

"And I'll bet your funding comes from one of those companies," Bess said brightly.

Edberg smiled at Bess. "Smart girl! What did you say your name is?"

When Bess told him, he said, "Well, Bess, I hope you sign up for one of my classes next semester. And you, too—"

"Nancy. Nancy Drew."

"Nancy. It's a pleasure talking to bright, interested students. Actually my research is funded by one of the leaders in the 'human potential movement,' a company based right here in Emersonville. It's called Positive Tapes."

Nancy quickly wrote down the name. "This is going to make a great story," she fibbed. "Do you think we could visit Positive Tapes to get their viewpoint?"

Professor Edberg was only too happy to help. While the girls sat with him, he called the president of Positive Tapes, a man named Larry Boyd, and made an appointment for Nancy and Bess to interview him in an hour. Then he gave them directions to the company's office in downtown Emersonville.

"I must tell you this interview has been a most enjoyable distraction from this horrible murder business," he told them, glancing at his watch. "Unfortunately, I have another class to teach, so we'll have to cut our conversation short."

"We understand, Professor," Nancy assured him. "You've been very helpful. Thank you." She and Bess rose to leave. They were already at the door when Nancy was struck by a sudden thought.

"Just one thing, Professor," she said, pausing. "I know we left the subject of the Wayne Perkins murder way behind, but where were *you* at the time of the killing?"

His expression darkened suddenly. "I beg your pardon? Are you suggesting *I* had something to do with the murder?" he demanded sharply.

Nancy realized she had gone too far. "Oh, no, of course not," she said instantly. To her relief his flash of anger faded.

"The police said Wayne was killed at around seven last night, yes? I live quite close to campus—I must have been home for well over an hour by then. You'd have to ask my wife. She keeps track of these things for me. You know us professors, always lost in the clouds. Now, I really must go."

Professor Edberg stood, pulled on his coat, and

picked up his briefcase. He escorted the girls out and closed the office door. Bess eyed the professor's coat.

"Aren't all the psych classes in this building?" she asked.

"I'm team-teaching a 'Literature and Psychology' class with Dr. Yannopoulos from the English department," Professor Edberg explained. "You should take it sometime. 'Bye now." With that, he dashed off toward the stairs.

"You were laying it on a bit thick there, Marvin," Nancy said when he was gone. "'Oh Professor, that's so fascinating,'" she mimicked, then giggled.

"He ate it up," Bess added and grinned.

"What did you think of him?" Nancy asked as the two girls headed down the stairs.

Bess twisted a strand of blond hair absentmindedly around a finger. "He's cute, kind of like a teddy bear," she decided.

A blast of frigid air hit them as they stepped outside. Ahead of them they could see Professor Edberg, hunched against the cold as he headed for a building that was across a small lawn.

Nancy paused as she spotted an athletic figure running toward the professor from across the yard. At first she thought it was just a student out jogging. Then the runner let out a shout, and Edberg turned toward him, startled.

"Oh, no!" Nancy shouted, as she recognized the figure. "It's Parker!"

Nancy and Bess hurried down the steps of the

psych building and ran toward Parker, but Parker was faster. He vaulted effortlessly over a hedge that stood between him and Edberg. Nancy watched in horror as Parker grabbed the professor by the lapels of his overcoat. The distraught young man slammed Professor Edberg up against the trunk of a great oak tree.

"Edberg!" he snarled, his face just inches from the professor's. "My lawyer told me about the pack of lies you told the police. You're going to pay for that!"

Chapter

Seven

PARKER'S GONE CRAZY!" Bess exclaimed. "We've got to stop him before he hurts Professor Edberg!" She continued toward Parker and the professor, but Nancy grabbed her arm.

"No! Look—here comes Ned!"

Sure enough, Ned and several other fraternity brothers came running after Parker. They caught up to him and pulled him away from Dr. Edberg.

"Parker, come on now, take it easy! You're only making things worse this way!" Nancy heard Ned say.

"Shouldn't we still go to him?" Bess asked. "He looks really upset!"

The girls were several yards away, and Nancy wanted to keep it that way. "The guys will calm him down. I don't want Edberg to connect us with Parker."

The two girls hung back by another tree, watching and listening. Parker strained against his friends, trying to get at Edberg.

"You don't understand!" Parker raved. "He's trying to make me look guilty! He told the police that I had a grudge against Wayne and that he thought I was dangerous!"

"And you're proving it all now, aren't you!" Edberg shouted, pointing a finger at Parker.

Just then a campus patrol car pulled up. Captain Backman emerged and ambled over to Edberg and the boys. "Is there a problem here?" he asked.

"This young hothead just assaulted me!" Edberg said, pointing at Parker.

"Why did you do that, son?" Backman spoke soothingly, but there was an underlying command in his voice.

Suddenly Parker's shoulders slumped, and he looked sheepish. "I—I don't know," he muttered. "This murder charge is driving me crazy. My lawyer told me some stuff, and I guess I started blaming my troubles on Professor Edberg."

Edberg had regained his composure and now looked at Parker with a sympathetic expression. "That's a common psychological mechanism called transference, Parker. You need someone to blame, and I'm an easy target."

"Do you really believe I killed Wayne?" Parker looked at Edberg imploringly.

"I was grief stricken and angry when I spoke to the police," Edberg admitted. "Perhaps I should have measured my words more carefully."

Backman spoke up. "You know, son, if the professor here presses assault charges, your bail will be revoked. You could go to jail until your trial, which might be weeks or even months away."

Edberg assured them that he wouldn't press charges. "Parker has enough troubles without my contributing to them. I'll let it go this time."

Parker thanked him and apologized for his behavior. Then his friends led him away. A moment later Professor Edberg continued along the path toward a building opposite the psychology building.

Nancy exchanged a look with Bess. "Phew! That was intense—"

"Ah, Miss Drew," a deep voice called.

Looking over, Nancy saw that Captain Backman was approaching them.

"A student named Janis Seymour called the Campus Safety office about you," Captain Backman went on. "She said you were asking a lot of questions."

Nancy started to respond, but Backman held up his hand. "I don't mind your doing a little investigating. In fact, your talents might prove helpful on this case. But I think Lieutenant Easterling would disagree. He'll come down hard if he thinks you're meddling in his case. Tread lightly, Nancy, and make certain you don't get into trouble yourselves. Is that clear?"

"Very clear," Nancy assured him. She gave him a questioning look. "As long as you're here, would you mind answering a couple of questions?"

Backman let out a deep, rolling laugh. "You're a born detective, young lady. Ask away!"

"We've heard that the murder weapon belonged to Parker's father."

"That's right. The police are checking to see if it has been reported stolen, although that would be quite a coincidence."

Nancy had to agree with that. Besides, Parker had said himself that he'd been at his parents' house just the weekend before. Changing the subject, she said, "About Dr. Edberg—"

"He has a rock-solid alibi," Captain Backman told her. "His wife told the police he was singing in the shower at seven—right when Perkins was being killed. She was very certain of the time. Besides, what motive would he have for killing his most trusted assistant?" He shook his head and added, "I'm afraid things don't look good for your friend."

"Nancy has broken cases that seemed a lot tighter!" Bess put in hotly. "Nobody's proved anything against Parker yet. Besides, what motive would Parker have for killing Wayne?"

"That's for the police to decide," Backman replied. "From what I hear, Perkins was constantly on his case. Maybe Parker just couldn't take the pressure anymore." He paused thoughtfully. "Now I have a campus to tend to, so I'd better be off. Keep me posted about what you find out."

Nancy and Bess assured him that they would, and he drove off.

"Hey," Nancy said, glancing at her watch. "We have an appointment to keep at Positive Tapes. If we don't hurry, we'll be late!"

Positive Tapes was located in downtown Emersonville, just off the row of stores and restaurants that lined the main street. Nancy parked her Mustang in front of a remodeled three-story brick building that looked as if it had once been a school. Several neon yellow vans, all sporting the Positive Tapes logo, were parked in a lot next to the building.

After stopping on Main Street for a quick slice of pizza, the girls headed for the entrance of the Positive Tapes building. "Let's see what this place is all about," Nancy said.

The interior of the building had been decorated in a completely modern style. The walls and ceiling of the lobby were painted a soft, pale rose. The carpeting and all the furnishings were charcoal colored. Plants and sculptures added to the decor. The effect was striking, Nancy had to admit.

As Nancy and Bess entered, they saw a pretty girl with frizzy hair. She was sitting at a high-tech workstation, complete with intercom and TV monitors that showed various parts of the building and its grounds.

"Hi," she greeted Nancy and Bess. "You must be Miss Drew and Miss Marvin. I'm Margie. Have a seat. I'll tell Dad, er, Mr. Boyd that you're here." She pressed a button on her console. A green light flashed, and she spoke into the intercom. "They're here."

Before the girls could settle into two of the comfortable chairs in the reception area, a beaming, youthful-looking man in his midforties bounded out to greet them. He was just under six feet tall, with thick black hair that was elaborately swept back. He was wearing a bright plaid jacket and navy pants.

"Hello, girls! Larry Boyd here," he greeted them, shooting them an electrifying smile. "Glad you could make it. You got lucky, I have an open half hour. You don't know how hard it is to grab a minute around here. So what can I do you for?"

Nancy shook Boyd's hand mutely, feeling overwhelmed by his verbal barrage. He looked like a man who never stopped smiling. As Boyd ushered her and Bess into his office, Nancy said, "We were very interested in Dr. Edberg's project. We thought we could do a story about subliminals for the school newspaper."

"It's great stuff, let me tell you. This field has a big, bright future, and here at Positive Tapes we're right on the cutting edge. Have a seat."

He gestured to a couch that faced his chrome

and glass desk. The stark white wall behind Boyd was covered with framed photographs of him posing with famous actors, politicians, and athletes.

When the girls were seated, Larry Boyd leaned over his desk and lowered his voice to a stage whisper. "Did you know that most people use only one tenth of their brainpower? It's a fact! All that human potential waiting to be unlocked—and we have the key!"

Nancy exchanged a quick look with Bess. Was this guy for real?

Boyd grabbed a tape off his desk and held it up for them to see. The title on its label was, Be Smoke-Free in a Week!

He jumped back up to his feet. "Come with me!" he said, and strode out of the room without a backward glance.

Nancy shrugged at Bess, then the two girls hurried to follow him. "Hold my calls, Margie," Boyd remarked as he zipped by the receptionist. He led the girls into a mirrored elevator off the lobby and pushed the button for the third floor. "That's where our recording studios are," he explained.

They emerged on the third floor, and Larry Boyd led them down a gray-carpeted hallway. There were a dozen doors along the hallway, each one leading to a state-of-the-art recording studio. After directing the girls into an empty studio, Boyd sat at a console and popped the tape into a cassette deck.

"Just listen to this," he said.

The studio had a spectacular speaker system, Nancy realized as sounds of the sea filled the room. She could just picture gentle breakers rolling up onto a sandy beach. There were the cries of sea gulls and then a beautiful, gentle melody played on a harp.

"It's beautiful," Bess commented. "But how does it make people stop smoking?"

"Listen." Boyd turned some dials, and the music faded away. The sound of a voice rose up, until they could hear it clearly. Nancy recognized Larry Boyd speaking softly and soothingly.

"I am a healthy, beautiful human being. My body is pure, clean. I have no desire to fill it with smoke. My need for cigarettes is falling, falling away. I feel a deep, inner peace."

The voice went on, but Larry Boyd turned the dials again, and the voice faded until once again there was only the music and the sound of the sea.

"That works?" Bess asked, looking amazed.

"You bet it does!" Boyd asserted, smiling broadly.

"But you don't have any proof of that," Nancy pointed out.

"Until now," he corrected her. "Thanks to Aaron Edberg, we're on the verge of clinical proof. I've built a nice little business here. We have a thriving mail-order operation, and our tapes are in bookstores and music shops all over the country. But now we're ready to take the next step—"

"Dr. Edberg said the government is interested in subliminal tapes," Bess put in.

"That's right. But there's heavy pressure from the government to demonstrate that these things work."

Nancy hesitated slightly before asking, "What if they *don't* work?"

Boyd frowned. "That, young lady, is the downside. There are government regulators who want to put controls on the claims we can make for our tapes and even on the types of tapes we can sell. That's a problem!" He sighed theatrically, then brightened. "But with the great results Aaron Edberg has been getting . . ."

Nancy didn't trust Larry Boyd, but she wasn't sure how he might have been involved in Wayne's murder. "Does Wayne Perkins's murder interfere with your plans at all?" she asked.

"What a terrible tragedy. Sure it does," Boyd replied. "That boy was very important to Aaron. I don't know what effect his death will have on Aaron's research. Frankly, I'm a bit worried."

"Did you know Wayne?" Bess asked.

Larry Boyd shook his head. "Afraid not. I never met him. I tried to keep a hands-off policy—didn't want to be accused of trying to influence the results of the study. It's a funny thing. I've lived in Emersonville all my life, but I've never been out to the college."

Nancy looked over as the door to the studio

opened and Margie entered with a tray on which were a pot of tea, a sugar and creamer, and three cups. "I thought you might want a little something to warm you up," she said.

Larry Boyd was certainly a charmer, Nancy thought as she and Bess gratefully accepted the hot tea from Margie. What she still didn't know was whether or not he had been involved in a murder.

After taking a sip of her tea, Nancy asked, "So you weren't anywhere near campus last night?"

"No, ma'am!" Boyd laughed. "Margie, hon, where was I last night?"

"Where you are every night, Dad. Right here," she answered.

"That's right!" he said. "I get here at seven in the morning, stay till nine every night!"

Nancy and Bess asked some more questions while they finished their tea but didn't find out anything more specific about Professor Edberg's study or about how Larry Boyd might fit into Wayne's murder.

"Mr. Boyd, this has been fascinating, but we really shouldn't take up any more of your time," Nancy finally said, getting to her feet.

"Yes. Thank you so much," Bess added.

Larry Boyd and Margie accompanied them back to the lobby. As Nancy and Bess headed for the door, Boyd insisted that they take a copy of the Positive Tapes promotional brochure. On its cover was a glossy color photograph of Larry Boyd's smiling face.

"Mr. Enthusiasm," Bess muttered when they were back in Nancy's car. "Do you think he's for real?"

Nancy shrugged. "I think he's a great salesman, but whether or not he believes his own hype is hard to say."

"What were you getting at with those questions about Wayne?" Bess asked.

"I was just probing a little. I wanted to see if he had anything to gain from Wayne's death," Nancy explained.

"And?"

"It sounded like just the opposite, as if Wayne's death could actually hurt his study. Still, I'd like to know more about Larry Boyd."

"How do we do that?"

"He said he's lived here all his life," Nancy said, starting the engine. "Somebody with that much personality is sure to get his name in the local paper now and then. Let's go take a look."

The Emersonville public library had a complete set of the Emersonville *Gazette* on microfilm going back fifty years. Nancy and Bess took a tray of tapes covering the past twenty-five years and set themselves up in front of a pair of microfilm reading machines. They started with the annual indexes, searching for anything on Larry Boyd or Positive Tapes, Inc.

Recent issues of the paper were full of items about Boyd and his company. Positive Tapes was one of the town's leading employers, the girls discovered, and Larry Boyd was one of Emersonville's biggest boosters. He was a member of the Chamber of Commerce, the Lions Club, the Rotary, and he was a town councilman. From all that the girls read, he was a pillar of the community.

But earlier editions of the paper told a different story about Mr. Boyd. There was the legal trouble fifteen years ago, when Boyd had run a practice as an unlicensed hypnotherapist. And a few years before that he had had his insurance license revoked when he forged a client's signature.

"Look at this," Nancy said in a hushed tone as she fed yet another roll of microfilm into the machine. Bess squeezed in next to her to look at the screen.

The issue of the *Gazette* on the screen was from twenty years earlier. A front-page photograph showed a much-younger Larry Boyd being led from the courthouse by two officers. He wasn't smiling.

Bess gasped as she read the caption beneath the photo: "'Lawrence Boyd Delbert sentenced to five years in the state penitentiary for manslaughter'!"

Chapter

Eight

Nancy let out a low whistle. "I'll bet this isn't in Boyd's official biography," she said.

Bess frowned at the photograph. "Do you think this means that Boyd killed Wayne Perkins? I mean, if he killed before, maybe he's capable of doing it again."

"It's not that simple, Bess," Nancy said. "This still doesn't prove a connection between him and Wayne's murder." She bent closer to the screen. "Here, let's read the article. Larry Boyd was in his early twenties. It was a barroom brawl, the other guy pulled out a knife. Boyd struggled with him, and the other guy was the one who ended up stabbed. Boyd was sentenced to two years in prison. There's no indication that he ever committed a violent crime again."

Nancy sighed and turned to Bess. "So we've learned that Larry Boyd is, or used to be, pretty sleazy. We've got to include him in our suspect list, despite his alibi. But until we find some hard, fast evidence linking him to Wayne's murder, we have only our suspicions."

"So what's our next step?" Bess asked.

"We still need to interview Diana DeMarco," Nancy said. "But first I'd like to learn more about Wayne Perkins. Maybe that way we can find a motive for someone besides Parker to want him dead."

"I don't get it, Nan," Bess said, an hour and a half later. "Why is it so hard to learn anything about Wayne?"

"I don't know," Nancy confessed. The two girls were sitting on a bench outside the psychology building, watching a squirrel forage through the snow. Nancy hoped the cold air would help her to think more clearly.

After leaving the local library, she and Bess had gone first to the campus security office and then to Wayne Perkins's office. They hadn't found out much about him at either place. He had received his undergraduate degree from a university on the East Coast, graduating with honors. His application to Emerson specified that he was interested in working with Edberg. As for family, Wayne had none. Both parents were deceased, and he had no brothers or sisters. He'd apparently been on his own for years.

The two other graduate students who shared Wayne's office in the psychology building hadn't been able to add much to that. Wayne had kept to himself, didn't talk much about his work. They weren't aware of any enemies Wayne might have had.

"What about that girl the other graduate students mentioned?" Bess now asked. "They said they saw Wayne with her off campus a few times."

Nancy nodded. "They said she was a brunette. It could be Diana DeMarco," she said. "We really need to talk to her, but it's almost dinnertime. Right now I think we should head over to the fraternity house and see how the guys are doing."

They arrived just in time for dinner. Four of the brothers were bustling around in the big community kitchen, cooking a huge batch of fried chicken and mashed potatoes. The boys readily made room for Nancy and Bess at the dining room table.

"Where's Parker?" Bess asked, looking around the table.

"He's upstairs, sleeping," Ned explained. "He crashed after that run-in with Edberg."

Dave Webb served himself some chicken, then passed the platter to Nancy. "I just hope he wakes up in time for our meeting tonight."

"There's a meeting in the living room in an hour," Ned explained to the girls. "It's about tomorrow's party. I'm sure no one would object to you two sitting in."

An hour later, dinner was finished and the kitchen squad was busy washing pots, pans, and dishes. Word of the meeting had spread among the fraternity brothers, and now they began to drift into the living room.

Before the meeting started, Nancy found Diana DeMarco's phone number in the student directory, but her call was answered by a machine. Nancy left a message for Diana to call her at Omega Chi, then joined the others in the common room.

Soon after she'd squeezed into a chair next to Ned, Parker came in. As the brothers murmured greetings and encouragement, Bess walked over and gave him a warm hug. They sat together on one of two old couches arranged around the big stone fireplace. At last nearly everyone involved in putting on the party was present, about ten brothers in all. Howie Little, who was fraternity president, called the meeting to order.

"I'm sure that by now you're all aware of Parker's legal difficulties," he said to the group. This was greeted by several calls of "Hang in there, Parker," and "We're with you, pal."

"I'm glad to see that we all understand the meaning of brotherhood here," Howie continued. "Because first and foremost we *are* a brotherhood, and what happens to one happens to all of us. In view of this crisis, several brothers have

73

suggested that maybe we should cancel tomorrow night's party. We've decided to put it to a committee vote. Does anyone have anything to say?"

Several hands shot up. Some of the guys argued that the seriousness of Parker's situation made them feel uncomfortable about partying. Others, Ned among them, felt that changing their plans would look bad to the college community and that they should go ahead with the party. Listening to them all, Nancy felt as if she were watching true democracy at work.

At last Parker rose to speak. He was a bit choked up, but he finally managed to say, "You guys are the best. I can't tell you how much your support means to me. As most of you know, I—I don't have a clear recollection of what happened last night. But I swear to you, I didn't kill anybody." He smiled at Nancy. "Nancy Drew is going to prove that."

The group gave Nancy a big cheer, and Nancy smiled uncomfortably. As time went on, she felt more and more certain that Parker *was* innocent. But all the evidence continued to point his way. If she didn't come up with a lead soon, Parker could end up going to jail!

Nancy pushed the thought from her mind and continued to listen to Parker.

"I want you guys to know that, since I didn't do anything wrong, we have nothing to be ashamed of. I think it's important that we have our party tomorrow, and I vote in favor!"

This last statement was greeted by applause,

hoots, and whistles of approval. When the rest of the group voted, the decision was unanimous: The party would proceed as planned.

As the meeting broke up, Nancy noticed that Parker and Bess stayed behind on the couch. She and Ned went over and joined them.

"Sorry to interrupt, but I have to ask you some questions, Parker," Nancy said.

Parker nodded. "Sure. Bess has just been filling me in on what you guys found out today."

"Can you tell me about your father's gun?" Nancy asked.

Parker suddenly looked down at his lap. "Uh, it wasn't exactly Dad's gun anymore. He's a collector—he's got dozens of guns in display cases. But he gave me that little thirty-eight snub-nose for my eighteenth birthday. We just hadn't gotten around to changing the registration." Parker paused before adding, "It's my gun."

"Your gun! Oh, Parker, how could you overlook something like that? Have you told the police?" Nancy was becoming exasperated. Every time she began to believe in Parker's innocence, some new bombshell made him look even more guilty.

Parker's green eyes darted around. "I—I just remembered," he said, looking confused. "It's weird. It's as if I didn't even remember owning it until just now! I keep the gun locked up in my desk drawer at home. At least, I did."

He was becoming more flustered, so Nancy

decided not to press him anymore. "You're going to have to let the police know about this in the morning," she said. "Meanwhile, why don't you relax? You and Bess could go see a movie or something."

Parker looked questioningly at Bess, and she nodded her agreement. "Okay," he agreed. "Anything but a murder mystery! What are you going to do?"

"I have an idea," Nancy said, turning to Ned. "I'll need your help."

"You think he's guilty, don't you?" Ned asked.

Nancy was hurt by his accusing tone. "I don't know what to think," she said truthfully. "One moment I think he's the nicest, most open guy in the world, and the next I think it might all be an act. You've got to admit his behavior is very odd."

It was after eleven in the evening, and the two of them were sitting in her blue Mustang, parked on a darkened residential street several blocks from campus.

"He *is* acting weird," Ned agreed. "It's a side of him I never saw before yesterday. At least keep an open mind, okay?"

Nancy kissed Ned's cheek. "That's why we're here," she told him.

She glanced across the street at the single-story green building where Wayne had lived. It was in a neighborhood of rundown houses near the campus—the student rental district, Ned had explained. The house was roped off with police tape, but Nancy wasn't going to let that stop her.

"If you see anything suspicious, beep the horn twice," she told Ned. When he nodded, she slipped quietly out of the car, leaving him sitting behind the wheel of her Mustang.

Nancy had gone back to the dormitory and changed into black jeans and a dark, hooded sweatshirt. Now she crossed the street and slipped around to the side of the house. She tested all the windows, until at last she found a basement one that opened. She took a deep breath, then climbed through, dropping several feet to the floor.

Nancy had brought a penlight with her, and she shone it around her briefly. The basement was a mess, full of boxes and piles of books. Before going through those things, however, she wanted to examine the rooms where Wayne had spent most of his time. Moving as silently as she could, Nancy picked her way carefully to the stairs on the other side of the basement.

For a moment she stopped, holding her breath. Had she heard the floor above her creak? She listened, her heart pounding, but heard nothing more. It must have been the house settling, she decided.

Nancy climbed the stairs and stepped into a tiny kitchen with dirty dishes still piled up in the sink. The kitchen led to a small living room full of musty furniture. There were bookshelves and file cabinets everywhere, and a computer sat on a desk.

Nancy played her penlight over the papers piled on the desk. She would definitely check those out as soon as she'd made a quick survey of the house.

She tiptoed across the living room to another doorway, which she guessed must lead to the bedroom. After carefully pushing the door open, she took a step in. It was pitch-black.

A sudden sound behind Nancy made her whirl around. She flicked on her penlight—and gasped.

A shadowy figure lurking behind the door was swinging a heavy bowling trophy right at Nancy's head!

Chapter

Nine

Nancy reacted instantly. She ducked, and the swinging trophy swooshed harmlessly past her ear.

Lashing out with her hand, Nancy caught her attacker's wrist. She pivoted, twisting the person's arm over her shoulder and following through with a judo throw that carried the shadowy figure right over her.

The attacker sprawled awkwardly on the floor. A quick glance told Nancy that it was a girl about her own size. In a flash, Nancy pinned the other girl's arms in a judo hold. With her free hand, Nancy reached out and found her penlight, which she had dropped during the attack. She flicked it on and shone the beam in the other girl's face.

"Diana DeMarco!" she exclaimed. "I've been looking for you all day, and now I find you here, trying to kill me!"

"I was not!" the pretty, dark-haired girl protested.

Nancy looked at her dubiously. "Then why did you attack me?"

"I heard you coming up the stairs and got scared. I thought you were Wayne's killer! I was just protecting myself. Now let me go—you're hurting me!"

Nancy released her grip, and Diana got to her feet. "Who are you, anyway? Why are you here, and how do you know who I am?"

"I think I'm the one who should be asking the questions," Nancy said, "but I'm Nancy Drew. I saw you talking to Wayne in the student union yesterday shortly before he was killed. I'm trying to find out who killed Wayne and why. Now, what are *you* doing here?"

As Diana brushed her hair from her eyes, Nancy appraised her. She was nearly as tall as Nancy. Her blue ski jacket was open over a gray bodysuit and tight black denim pants that she wore with boots.

"I—I was looking for something," Diana told her, glancing nervously around.

Nancy crossed her arms over her chest. "Why don't you try telling me what it is?"

A look of embarrassment crossed Diana's face. "I did something terribly wrong," she said after a long pause. "I was Wayne's student, and I was dating him." She took a deep breath, and then her words came out in a rush. "I knew it was against school regulations, but I couldn't help it—I really liked Wayne. He resisted at first, but I kept after him. Finally he gave in, and we started seeing each other secretly."

"Yes?" Nancy prompted. Diana still hadn't said what she was doing here.

"But then, when he was killed," Diana went on, "I knew I could get into big trouble if anyone found the love notes I'd sent him. I knew where he kept his spare key, so I came here looking for them."

"Did you find them?" Nancy asked.

Diana nodded and reached into her coat pocket. "Careful," Nancy warned, fearing that Diana might have a concealed weapon. "Move slowly."

The other girl eased a little packet out of her pocket and held it up so Nancy could see it wasn't a weapon. Nancy took the packet from her, opened it, and gave a couple of the notes a quick reading. They were romantic and passionate, and Nancy felt awkward reading them. Still, there might be something useful in them. For the moment, she decided to hang onto the letters.

"You must be taking Wayne's death pretty hard," she said sympathetically.

Diana didn't reply right away, and Nancy saw that she was blinking back tears. Then Diana asked, "What did you mean when you said you're trying to find out who killed Wayne? I thought the police had proof that Parker Wright did it."

"You know Parker from your study sessions. Do you think he's capable of murder?"

"It *is* hard to believe," Diana admitted. "But then, who?"

"That's what I'm trying to find out," Nancy said, tapping the letters against her palm. "If you have any information, you should go to the police."

Diana immediately became flustered. "No! I mean, I couldn't." She looked nervously around Wayne's darkened bedroom. "Listen, we'd better get out of here, or we'll both be in trouble! Please, let me have those letters back."

"I think I'll hold on to them," Nancy said coolly. She felt sure that Diana was hiding something, and she was determined to find out what it was.

"I don't think you should," Diana said, her voice hardening. "Look, we can't just stand around here chatting. I saw a police car cruise by, just before I entered. The police could be back at any moment."

"I still have a lot of questions I want to ask you," Nancy said.

"Fine. I'll answer them—but not here." Diana reached out and snatched the letters from Nancy's grasp. Before Nancy could react, Diana walked out of the bedroom. "We can have breakfast together at nine o'clock," Diana called over her shoulder. "Meet me in my dorm room." Then she was gone.

Nancy felt a surge of frustration. She didn't trust Diana, but there was really no way she could force her to stay and talk.

Nancy was about to continue her search of the house, when she noticed an envelope lying on the floor of Wayne's bedroom. It must have fallen out of Diana's pocket when Nancy threw her down. Was it another love letter? She picked it up and opened it.

The envelope contained two small computer diskettes. She'd have to wait until later to examine them, though. For now, she wanted to finish looking around and get out of here. If Diana had been telling the truth about the police circulating, she didn't want to get caught!

As Nancy slipped the envelope into the pocket of her jeans, she felt the glossy coating of the Positive Tapes pamphlet Larry Boyd had given her earlier. She made a quick search of the rest of the house but didn't turn up anything that could be a clue to who Wayne's murderer was. Ten minutes later, Nancy left, slipping out the kitchen door and carefully replacing the police tape across the doorway.

Since she didn't want to be spotted by any patrol cars, she sneaked through the yard next door, then crossed the street a few houses down. She approached the Mustang quietly, on the passenger side. Ned was staring intently at Wayne's house and didn't realize that Nancy was there until she flung open the door and popped into the car. "Boo!" she said. "Miss me?"

Ned jerked around, startled. Then he started to laugh. "Who taught you to sneak around like that?"

"Years of practice, Nickerson," she responded, giving him a quick kiss.

"Find anything?"

Nancy nodded. "Diana DeMarco," she replied. Before Ned could ask anything more, she said, "I'll tell you all about it. But right now let's get out of here. The cops might be patrolling this street."

Ned started Nancy's car and pulled away from the curb. Before they reached the end of the block, a police car rounded the corner, then drove past them, headed in the direction of Wayne's house. Nancy gave a sigh of relief. It had been that close.

As they drove back to the Emerson campus, she told Ned about her encounter with Diana.

"They were actually dating?" Ned asked, looking surprised. When Nancy nodded, he added, "So do you think *she* could have killed him?"

Nancy grew thoughtful. "It's possible, though I don't know what motive she could have. She seemed genuinely upset by Wayne's death, but I had a definite feeling she was hiding something." She reached into her pocket and pulled out the envelope Diana had dropped. "Maybe these will help." She told Ned about the diskettes and how she'd found them.

"What's on them?" he wondered.

"I don't know. I didn't get a chance to look." She opened the envelope and took out the diskettes, then read the hand-lettered labels. "Hey, this might be important!"

Ned glanced over from the driver's seat. "What've you got?"

"This one is labeled Subliminal Persuasion: Analysis and Assessment," Nancy told him. "I think these are the records of Professor Edberg's study!"

"I'm glad Parker and Bess had a good time at the movies," Nancy said two hours later as she and Ned walked down the upstairs hall of the Omega Chi Epsilon house. They'd just knocked on Parker's door and found him half-asleep. He woke up long enough to tell them that after the movie, he had dropped Bess off at Packard Hall, then returned to the fraternity.

"Let's just hope Maury is having some luck with those diskettes so that we can all get some sleep," Ned said. He pushed into a tiny bedroom that was filled with computer equipment. A narrow bed was squashed against one wall, as if it were an afterthought.

"This is interesting," Maury Becker said, looking up from his computer screen. Immediately after leaving Wayne's house, Nancy and Ned had gone back to the fraternity to show Maury the diskettes Nancy had found. He'd immediately agreed to examine them. Then Nancy and Ned had gone out to get something to eat so that Maury would be able to concentrate, without the two of them hovering over him.

"It took a few tries to find which word-processing program Edberg was using," Maury now said. "After that it was a breeze to access his file menu. It's going to take time to examine them, but it looks like this first disk, the one labeled Subliminal Persuasion, contains records of Professor Edberg's study."

Nancy leaned over Maury's shoulder and peered at the screen. "What about the other disk?" she asked. "The one labeled Reevaluation?"

Maury frowned. "That one's proving more difficult to access," he explained. It's been blocked—a coded input sequence is required in order to access the files."

"In English, please, Maury," Ned interrupted. "We're not all computer experts."

"Okay, look. You boot up the computer, it asks you what you want to do. You tell it the program you want to use, and then the computer reads the diskette," Maury explained. "This block is preventing me from getting into the disk to read what's on it. Unless you tell the computer the secret code, it won't open the files. It's a security device."

"So someone wanted to keep the information on this second disk secret," Nancy said.

"That's right," Maury answered.

Nancy felt herself growing excited. "This information could be the key to Wayne Perkins's murder!" she said. "Are you sure we can't access the information?"

"Oh, ye of little faith," Maury said, smiling up at her. "That would be impossible only if Wayne was a better programmer than I am. But *nobody* is a better programmer than I am!"

Ned put his arm around Maury's shoulders. "And that's why we love you, Maury. Who could resist such modesty? How long do you think it will take until you break into this disk?"

"Not long. A day. Maybe a day and a half," he said distractedly, his attention already refocused on his work. "Come back Sunday morning after breakfast. I should have it by then."

"Yikes!" Nancy said, glancing at her watch. "It's already two in the morning."

Ned yawned. "I'm beat. Come on. Let's get you to the dorm."

"I can't wait to meet this elusive Diana DeMarco," Bess said the next morning as they left their dorm room.

It was just before nine o'clock. Nancy had already been up for an hour, despite having gone to sleep so late. She couldn't stop thinking about the case. After dressing in white corduroy slacks and a blue sweater, she'd sat at one of the desks in her room, thinking over what she'd learned so far.

All the evidence pointed to Parker. He'd been with Wayne just before the murder, the gun was his, and he and the teaching assistant had been having problems. But then, Diana was hiding something, and she *had* been in the study group, too. And if Wayne had gone to the trouble of protecting information about the research, maybe the subliminal study was the key.

"I just hope Diana's there," Nancy said now, closing the door to their room behind them. "She's been pretty elusive so far."

The two girls went down a flight of stairs to the first floor, then made their way to Room 106. After several knocks, the door was opened, and Janis Seymour, wearing a nightgown and bathrobe, blinked at them.

"You again!" Janis said angrily. "What are you doing here so early?"

"I'm sorry if we woke you, Janis, but Diana asked me to meet her here at nine," Nancy said.

Janis stared at Nancy. "She didn't say anything to me. Anyway, she's gone."

"She's *gone?*" Nancy felt a terrible sinking feeling. She never should have trusted Diana! "Where did she go?"

Janis shrugged. "I heard her rattling around the room while it was still dark. I guess she was packing her bags. But I was half-asleep, and it didn't really register." Janis stepped back, showing Nancy and Bess Diana's side of the room.

Nancy couldn't believe her eyes. Diana's things had been completely cleared out!

Chapter

Ten

N**ANCY**, this is awful!" Bess cried, looking around the room in alarm.

Nancy groaned, mentally kicking herself for letting Diana convince her to wait until morning to interview her. "Listen, Janis, your roommate could be in real trouble. You've got to let us help her." She had a feeling that Diana was an important link to the case, and she had to find out where the dark-haired girl had gone.

"What kind of trouble?" Janis asked suspiciously. "Why should I believe you?"

Bess took Nancy's arm and started to pull her away. "She's right, Nancy, it's not our problem. Let Janis take the blame for whatever happens to her friend."

"Wait—wait a second," Janis called after them. They turned. "What can I do?" Janis asked.

Nancy and Bess stepped back into the room. "Just let us take a look around," Nancy said.

Soon she was giving the room a quick but thorough going over while Bess kept Janis distracted with small talk. Nancy looked for any clue that might tell her where Diana had gone, but the girl had left behind little more than an old towel, some cosmetics, and a few unimportant papers.

"How could she take everything?" Nancy wondered aloud.

"She never did have much," Janis answered. "Two suitcases and her laptop computer."

"For a whole school year?" Bess asked, looking doubtful. "That doesn't sound like much."

Nancy snapped her fingers. "Maybe she wasn't planning on staying for the whole year—"

She broke off as she spotted something in the wastebasket under Diana's desk. She pulled it out and saw that it was a small block of notepaper. There was a blue logo of a pair of headphones, with the name Subliminal Suggestions, Inc., printed beneath it. An address and phone number in Pittsburgh were also listed.

Nancy flipped through the pad, but there was nothing written on any of the sheets. Then she noticed that there were some faint indentations on the top sheet, and there was a ragged edge at the top, as if someone had torn off the sheet in haste. Taking a pencil out of the desk, Nancy began shading in the top sheet of the pad.

"Find something?" Bess asked, coming over.

Nancy showed her. The pencil shading highlighted the words that Diana had written on the pad: Mid-America Airlines, Flight 203, 10:15 A.M.

"She must be going home to Pittsburgh," Janis said, looking over Nancy's shoulder.

"We don't have much time," Nancy said. "Come on, Bess—" Then she stopped in her tracks. How could she have overlooked the obvious? Subliminal Suggestions had to be a rival of Positive Tapes! "Can I use this phone?" she asked Janis.

Janis nodded, and within seconds Nancy had dialed the number listed on the notepad. "Good morning, Subliminal Suggestions. How can we help you?" a receptionist's voice announced.

Nancy couldn't believe her luck. It was a stroke of good fortune that the company's office was open on Saturday. "May I speak with Diana DeMarco?" she asked.

"I'm sorry, Miss DeMarco is away on assignment. May I take a message?"

"No, I'll try later. Thanks." Nancy hung up the phone and grabbed Bess. Her heart was pounding with excitement. Finally she had a breakthrough! "Let's go!" she said, pulling her friend out the door.

"Can I ask what's going on?" Bess said, hurrying down the hall after Nancy. "Why are you so excited?"

"Diana DeMarco isn't really a student," Nancy told her. "She works for one of Larry Boyd's rivals. I bet anything she was here to steal information about Dr. Edberg's study. She's an industrial spy!"

Bess grabbed Nancy's arm. "Whoa, slow down! How do you know all this?"

When Nancy related her phone call to Subliminal Suggestions, Bess shook her head in amazement. "If she works for them, then she *can't* be a student. You must be right about her being a spy. I bet she was using Wayne to learn about the study. Maybe he found out that she was working for Subliminal Suggestions, threatened to expose her, and had to kill him!"

"I was thinking the same thing," Nancy said. "But what about Larry Boyd, not to mention the bald man Dave Webb saw at the psych building? Do they figure into this? We have lots of possibilities. Now we've just got to find out if any of these guesses are right or if Wayne died for some other reason entirely."

Soon after, the girls pulled into the Emersonville airport's parking lot. It was a small airport, with one medium-size terminal building, a control tower, and a single airstrip. Diana wouldn't be hard to find. After parking, the girls hurried into the terminal.

Nancy's gaze quickly scanned the people in

line at the two ticket counters. No Diana. "Come on!" she urged Bess, hurrying in the direction of the boarding gates.

As they approached the small line of people waiting to pass through the X-ray machine, Nancy spotted the familiar brown-haired figure. Diana was carrying two suitcases and her laptop computer.

"Diana! Hey, Diana, wait!" Nancy shouted.

A look of shock registered on Diana's face when she spotted Nancy. She tried to push past the other passengers, but the guard stopped her. Dropping her suitcases, she broke away from the line and ran down the hall away from the girls.

"I'm right behind you, Nan!" Bess called as Nancy took off after Diana.

A janitor was pushing a wet mop down the hallway. Diana tried to slow down as she hit the patch of damp tile floor, but she was too late. Her feet flew out from under her, and she fell with a thud. By the time she got to her feet, Nancy and Bess were glaring down at her.

"Why are you trying to get away?" Nancy demanded. "What have you got to hide?"

"I don't see that it's any of your business," Diana answered, getting to her feet and brushing off her slacks. "You have no right to try to stop me."

"Maybe I don't, but I'm sure the police will be interested in learning about your romance with Wayne. Your sudden departure will look pretty suspicious."

"I had nothing to do with his death!"

"Yeah, right," Bess scoffed. "We know all about how you're working for Subliminal Suggestions."

Diana shot a startled look at Bess. "How do you know about that?" she blurted out.

Suddenly all her bravado fell away, and Diana slumped in defeat. "What about the diskettes— did you find them?" she asked quietly. When Nancy nodded, Diana let out a sigh. "Maybe we should have breakfast together after all."

Soon the three girls were seated in the airport cafeteria, breakfasting on lukewarm coffee, orange juice, and stale rolls. Diana confirmed Nancy's guess that she was an industrial spy. "But Wayne wasn't my partner," she insisted. "He was one of the most honorable people I've ever met."

She took a sip of her coffee, then continued. "I graduated from college two years ago and went to work for Subliminal Suggestions. This fall I registered here under false pretenses. Right away I tried to get close to Wayne so I could learn about Edberg's study."

"And?" Bess prompted.

"Wayne resisted—he was very ethical. But I could tell he was attracted to me, and I kept after him. We finally started dating, but he still wouldn't tell me much, so this term I signed up for the study group."

"What happened the night he was killed?" Nancy asked. "Why was he so curt with you in the student union? Did he learn you were using him?"

Diana frowned down at her roll. "I don't know. He'd been acting distant for a few days. He was nervous, on edge. He said there were problems with the study, but he wouldn't say any more. I tried to confront him, and you saw how he reacted. That's all I know, but—" Diana hesitated.

"But what?" Nancy prodded.

Diana looked away for a moment and inhaled deeply. When she turned back, Nancy could see that her eyes were brimming with tears. "I really started to like him—a lot. And I can't help thinking that his death was somehow connected with Dr. Edberg's study. Did you find anything on those disks?"

"Not yet," Nancy said. "We're working on it." She just hoped they came up with some answers soon.

"I'm glad we were able to convince Diana to come back to Emerson," Bess said that evening as she and Nancy walked up the steps of the fraternity house. "I think she'll help us find the truth about Wayne's murder."

"Me, too," Nancy said as she knocked on the door. "I'm still not sure we can trust her, though. But her coming back on her own is a good sign."

After returning to the dormitory from the airport, Nancy and Bess had called Captain Backman and filled him in on what they'd learned about Diana DeMarco. He said that he'd pass the information along to Lieutenant Easterling. Now, as Nancy heard a fast song playing inside, she felt like forgetting all about the case. "Come on, Bess," she said. "Let's party!"

Soon after, Nancy and Ned were dancing in the fraternity's living room, in the midst of a big group of students. Rock music boomed out from the stereo system. Nearby, Howie Little and his girlfriend were dancing. Dave Webb bounced by with a pretty redhead and grinned at Ned and Nancy. Everyone was in high spirits. For the moment at least, all of Parker's problems were forgotten.

"This is the best party you guys have ever thrown!" Nancy shouted to Ned. She noticed that Parker was sitting with several of his friends, laughing and talking animatedly. Bess sat on the arm of his chair, and they were holding hands. Parker kept glancing appreciatively at Bess's black wool minidress and leggings. Nancy had to admit that Bess and Parker made a good-looking couple.

When the song ended, Nancy and Ned worked their way over to Parker and Bess. "How's it going?" Ned asked.

Parker smiled over at them. "Great! See, Nickerson—I told you we had to have this party."

The opening bars of the next song began to play, and Bess leapt to her feet. "Come on,

Parker, we have to dance. I love this song— 'Cosmic Mind Control'!" She pulled him to his feet.

Nancy grinned at Bess. "You can't get enough of Johnny Lightning and the Stormkings, can you?"

But Bess wasn't listening. She was staring at Parker in astonishment. "Parker? Are you okay? Parker?" she asked.

Looking at him, Nancy saw that his animated expression had disappeared. He just stood there next to Bess, his jaw slack and his eyes blank.

"Parker?" Ned said worriedly. He waved a hand in front of his friend's face, but Parker showed no reaction.

"Nancy!" Bess cried, looking horrified. "I think he's in some sort of trance!"

Chapter

Eleven

I'VE NEVER SEEN anything like this!" Nancy exclaimed. Several others gathered around Parker in concern. "Parker, can you hear me?" Nancy asked.

The young man didn't reply. He stood limply, his eyes glazed over, swaying slightly. Around them the party swirled. Most of the partygoers seemed unaware that anything was wrong.

"Let's get him somewhere quiet," Ned said, taking Parker by the arm. Parker followed blindly while Ned, Nancy, and Bess escorted him into the fraternity's study room, down the hall from the living room. Once he was away from the sounds of the music, Parker recovered almost immediately.

"Hey—where's the party? How did we get *here?*" He looked around in bewilderment.

"You don't remember?" Nancy asked.

Parker shook his head. "Remember what?"

"You blacked out again, Parker," Bess told him, her voice filled with concern.

"I did? But I felt fine. And then . . ." His voice trailed off. He sank into a comfortable chair and slumped forward, resting his head in his hands. "I don't know what's happening to me," he muttered. "I must be losing my mind!"

"I'll be right back," Ned told the girls. "Stay here with Parker."

He left the room, returning a few minutes later. "Let's get our coats," Ned told the others. "Dr. Cohen is going to meet us at the campus infirmary in ten minutes. He wants to take a look at you right away, Parker."

"I don't know what to tell you, Parker," Dr. Paul Cohen said an hour later.

Parker, Nancy, Bess, and Ned were sitting with the doctor in his small, plain office. He had spent the hour giving Parker a thorough physical, then asked them all to come into his office.

"There's nothing wrong with you that I can find," Dr. Cohen went on. "You're in top condition, and there's no obvious sign of neurological damage. We could schedule you for a CAT scan, I suppose." A thought occurred to him. "You haven't had any head injuries—a fall in gymnastics practice, anything of that sort?"

Parker looked up from the chair in which he was sitting. "No, nothing like that," he replied.

"Parker, did you tell the doctor about the psychological study you've been participating in?" Nancy suggested gently. "I think it might be important."

While Parker explained Dr. Edberg's study, Dr. Cohen listened closely. "So let me see if I've got this right," the doctor said when Parker finished. "For the past couple of months, you've listened to one of those subliminal tapes for an hour every week?"

Parker nodded.

"What did you think about while listening to the tapes?" Dr. Cohen asked.

"My mind would just kind of drift, you know? Sometimes I'd listen to the music. They tried different kinds." Parker smiled. "The last few weeks they were even using rock music."

That caught the doctor's interest. He turned to Nancy, Ned, and Bess. "This latest blackout happened at a party, right?" he asked. When they nodded, he added, "I have an idea. What song was playing when Parker blacked out?"

"It was a song from the new Johnny Lightning album," Bess replied.

Dr. Cohen's face lit up. "I have that here on tape!" he told them. "One of the nurses was listening to it on her Walkman, and she loaned it to me." He rummaged around in a desk drawer. "I like to keep up with music that students are listening to," Dr. Cohen explained. "Ah—here it is!" He held up a cassette. "Which track was it?"

"They were playing 'Cosmic Mind Control,'" Bess told him. "It's the best song on the album."

"And appropriate," Dr. Cohen joked. He popped the cassette into the portable tape player on his desk. "Let's give this rocker a listen," he said.

Sure enough, when he played the song, Parker once again went slack. He didn't seem to be aware of anything or anyone around him.

"Amazing!" Dr. Cohen exclaimed in a low voice. He turned the music off, and Parker began to blink and move around again.

"Is he going to be all right?" Bess asked, concerned.

"Just let him come out of it," Dr. Cohen advised. He bent over Parker, who was slumped forward in his chair. "Parker, how are you doing?" he asked softly.

Parker opened his eyes. He looked around and smiled at the others in the room. "I feel good. When are we going to listen to the song?"

Nancy gazed at Parker sympathetically. "We've already listened to it," she told him. "It stopped playing a few minutes ago."

Parker's smile faded, and he glanced around in confusion. "It—it happened again?" he asked.

"I'm afraid it's going to happen every time you hear this song," Dr. Cohen told him. "You've been hypnotized! This song is the trigger for a post-hypnotic suggestion. Whenever you hear it you go into a trance."

"What are you saying?" Parker demanded. He was starting to get agitated. "Are you telling me someone hypnotized me into shooting Wayne?"

The doctor was thoughtful. "I don't think so," he finally replied. "Most research on hypnosis indicates that it's impossible to get a person to do something they wouldn't normally do. But someone did have a reason to hypnotize you."

"We just met an expert in hypnotism yesterday," Bess put in.

"That's right! Parker, have you ever met a man named Larry Boyd?" Nancy asked. She wasn't sure how Boyd or Parker's hypnosis fit into Wayne's murder, but she had a strong hunch they were all connected.

"Larry Boyd? No. Who's he?" Parker asked.

"His company is funding the subliminal tapes study," Nancy explained. "He was once convicted of manslaughter. I consider him a suspect in Wayne's murder, but I haven't found any proof yet."

Ned looked questioningly at Dr. Cohen. "Do you know a lot about hypnosis?" he asked.

"Some," he answered. "In medical school I studied hypnosis technique for a term when I was considering specializing in psychiatry."

"Do you think you could 'undo' Parker's post-hypnotic suggestion?" Nancy asked. "Maybe then he'd remember everything."

"Well, it can be done," the doctor said. "I think I could do it. Still, you might be better off getting a real expert. We have one of the best hypnotherapists in the country right here at Emerson College."

Nancy leaned forward in her chair. "Really? Who is that?"

"His name is Edberg—Professor Aaron Edberg."

Nancy's mouth dropped open. "You're kidding!" she said, but the doctor's serious expression told her he wasn't.

Ned paced back and forth in front of Dr. Cohen's desk. "Boyd *and* Edberg," he murmured. "They're both involved in that subliminal tapes experiment—but which one would murder Wayne Perkins? And why?"

"Beats me," Nancy said. "That's been the problem all along—trying to come up with a motive for any of our suspects. For all we know, Diana DeMarco is a hypnotist, too."

"Come on, Nan. It's not her!" Bess exclaimed.

"Sorry, but I can't rule her out that easily. It's even possible that Wayne hypnotized Parker. He was an advanced graduate psych student—he probably knew how to."

"You don't really believe that," Bess protested.

"Maybe not. But we need to consider every possibility," Nancy said.

"So *why* was I hypnotized?" Parker spoke up.

Nancy shrugged. "Maybe so you could be used as the murder weapon."

"But we know he's incapable of murder—even under hypnosis!" Bess was becoming exasperated.

Dr. Cohen had been listening to the exchange with a look of fascination on his face. Now he joined in, saying, "Actually, whoever hypnotized you, Parker, wouldn't know whether or not you would really pull the trigger until the moment of truth arrived."

"Still, we need to come up with a motive that's more than guesswork," Nancy said. "Maybe Maury will have an answer for us in the morning when he finds out what's on the mystery diskette."

"How's it going, Maury?" Nancy asked, popping into Maury Becker's room.

It was early Sunday morning. Ned and Bess had gone with Parker to the infirmary, where Dr. Cohen was going to start breaking through the hypnosis. "I didn't see you at the party last night."

"That's because I was right here," he told her. "This is much more interesting. Pull up a chair."

Nancy sat next to Maury, and together they gazed at his computer screen. "Did you get through the block on the second disk?" Nancy asked.

Maury pointed across the room to another computer. Sequences of letters and numbers were flashing on its screen too rapidly for her to make them out. "My other system is still working on it," he told her. "I customized a program to test possible password sequences. The computer's been running them since midnight. It's tried a few million by now—we should be in soon. In the meantime, let me show you what's on this disk.

"Professor Edberg has been testing for statistically measurable learning improvement," Maury continued. "Some of his students get subliminal messages on their tapes. Others listen to tapes without subliminals, and some don't listen to tapes at all. But they all participate in the same study groups and take the same tests."

"So?" Nancy asked.

Maury pointed to the screen. "So it says here that the subliminals work. Edberg is almost done with his study, and he's had very good results."

Seeing the frown on Maury's face, Nancy said, "It sounds as if you're not so sure."

"Well, there's a lot of statistical stuff here that I haven't had a chance to examine, so I don't know yet if he's right or not," Maury said. "I've been checking out the files on individual students to see how he interpreted their results. Some of the reasoning is still confusing to me. I have to sort it out."

Nancy was starting to feel discouraged. So far he wasn't telling her anything that showed a motive for any of her suspects. "What about Parker's file—have you accessed it?"

"That's interesting, too," Maury said. "I haven't been able to locate it yet. Maybe there are files I still haven't accessed—"

"Hey, how's it going?" a new voice asked.

Nancy and Maury turned to see Dave Webb standing in the doorway, munching on an apple.

"They keep coming by," Maury explained to Nancy. "The whole house seems to have taken Parker on as their personal cause."

"Brotherhood is powerful," Dave agreed, ambling into the room. "Have you proved he's innocent yet?"

"I appreciate your faith in me, Dave," Maury answered, "but these things take time. You see—" He began to explain everything all over again, but Dave held up his hands and started to laugh.

"Whoa! I just need a simple answer." He looked around at the papers scattered on Maury's desk. Then his gaze fixed on the brochure Nancy had taken from Positive Tapes, half-buried among the pile of papers. She had pulled it out of her pocket when she gave Maury the diskettes and had forgotten it on his desk.

"Nancy! You found him!" Dave said.

Nancy gave him a puzzled glance. "What do you mean? Found who?" she asked, reaching for the brochure.

Dave pointed to the color photo of Larry Boyd on the cover. "He must be wearing a wig here," Dave answered. "But this is the bald guy I saw at the psych building the night Wayne was killed!"

Chapter

Twelve

O KAY, SO WHAT'S the plan again?" Dave asked a short while later. He and Nancy were sitting in Nancy's Mustang, which was parked outside a large split-level house in Emersonville's wealthiest neighborhood.

After checking the local phone book for Larry Boyd's home address, Nancy and Dave had driven right over. Nancy wanted Dave to get a face-to-face look at Boyd, to be absolutely positive that it was the same person he'd seen the night of Wayne's murder.

"I guess the easiest thing to do is simply ring the doorbell," Nancy said. "When we interviewed Boyd he insisted that he'd never been on campus. If you can identify him as the person who was in the psych building, then he was lying."

Dave nodded. "And the only reason he would lie is if he was up to no good—say, murdering Wayne Perkins." Dave let out a whistle, then reached for the door handle. "I'll try my best, Nancy."

They stepped out of the car. The morning air was crisp, but a hint of approaching spring hung in the air. Nancy and Dave were about to cross the street, when the front door of the house opened and a man stepped out. He was wearing a heavy robe and slippers. As he bent down to pick up the Sunday paper, Nancy saw that he had a fringe of hair around his temples, but the top of his head was completely bald. "That *is* Larry Boyd!" Nancy exclaimed. "But without hair."

"See? I told you it was him!" Dave declared excitedly. "I'm positive."

Larry Boyd must have heard Dave's enthusiastic outcry. He looked up and saw the two young people, and his face suddenly paled. He spun around quickly and hurried back into the house, slamming the door behind him.

Nancy and Dave stood on the sidewalk facing the house. "I didn't expect that reaction from him," Nancy confessed. "I wonder which one of us he's so scared of?"

"Beats me. What do we do now?" Dave asked.

"I still think we should try to talk to him." Squaring her shoulders, Nancy marched up the walk to Larry Boyd's house and rang the doorbell.

"Go away!" Boyd's voice came from behind the door.

"Mr. Boyd. I just want to talk to you," Nancy called out.

"I have nothing to say to you."

Nancy wasn't going to give up that easily. "You lied to me the other day when you said you'd never been on campus," she pressed.

"Go away or I'll call the police!"

"That's not a bad idea, Mr. Boyd. You have a lot to explain to them."

Nancy and Dave stayed on the front steps of the Boyd house, fruitlessly trying to get Larry Boyd to come out and talk with them. Soon a brown sedan pulled up to the curb, followed by a police car. Lieutenant Easterling climbed out of the sedan, and a pair of uniformed officers emerged from the patrol car. They stood by their car while Lieutenant Easterling approached the house.

"Lieutenant Easterling, I'm glad to see you," Nancy said.

"Is Lieutenant Easterling out there?" Boyd's voice came from behind the door. Then the door flew open, and Boyd rushed outside. "Lieutenant! This young woman is harassing me," he accused. "Arrest her!"

"What!" Nancy cried, astonished. "I am not!"

Easterling held up a hand. "Hold it, both of

you!" he ordered. He turned to Nancy. "Now, what's this all about? It's Sunday morning, and you're disturbing the peace and quiet of this man's home. What's your problem?"

"I'm investigating the Wayne Perkins murder, and I consider this man to be a prime suspect."

"You consider *me* a suspect!" Boyd sputtered, his face turning bright red. "How dare you!"

"Let me ask the questions here, okay?" the lieutenant said. "But he's got a good question, and I'll ask it," he went on, turning back to Nancy. "How dare you stick your nose in a police investigation? How dare you badger prominent citizens in *my* town?"

"But I'm not—"

"Oh, no? Didn't you tell both Mr. Boyd and Dr. Edberg that you're a reporter for the college newspaper? I got calls from both of them on Friday about you. You're not even a student there."

"I can explain."

Lieutenant Easterling brushed Nancy's explanation away. "Don't bother, I've heard it. You're an amateur detective, and you don't think the college boy shot his tutor, so you're looking for somebody else to pin it on. You think you've got evidence linking Boyd and Edberg to the crime, so that gives you the right to stick your nose where it doesn't belong?"

Nancy had heard about all she could take. "Wait just a minute," she said, glaring at him. "I have every right to try to get at the truth. And it so happens I *do* have several suspects besides Parker Wright, and I *have* found evidence linking others to the crime. If you'll just give me a minute to tell you what I've found—"

"Save it, kiddo. I don't want to hear the fantasies of a teenager with an overactive imagination!" The lieutenant's face was just inches from Nancy's. "I've been a cop for twenty-two years and a detective for the past fifteen. The last thing I need in the middle of a murder case is some kid who's supposed to be a hotshot detective telling me I don't know how to do my job!"

He took a deep breath, reining in his anger. "I'm going to say this just once: I've got a suspect, I've got motive, opportunity, and a murder weapon registered to the suspect's daddy with the suspect's prints all over it, and the suspect hasn't been able to offer even the lamest alibi. It's an open-and-shut case, and I want you to back off!"

Nancy stood her ground, struggling to control her anger. Glancing at Larry Boyd, she saw that he was standing with his arms folded across his chest, a smirk on his face. At last Nancy said, "Lieutenant, I'm trying to help your investigation, not hinder it. But if you can't see that—"

Dave Webb finally spoke up. "Save your breath, Nancy, this guy's not interested." He turned to Easterling. "But I'll tell you what, Lieutenant. I told you I saw a man in the psych building on Thursday night, and this is him." He pointed at Larry Boyd, who responded with a look of injured innocence. "Mr. Boyd told Nancy he'd never been on the Emerson College campus," Dave continued. "Maybe you've got the case pinned on Parker Wright, but if I were you I'd ask Mr. Boyd why he lied about that."

With that, Dave took Nancy's arm and led her toward her car. "Come on, let's let the police do their job." As they walked away, Lieutenant Easterling was eyeing Larry Boyd speculatively.

Nancy wished she and Dave could stay around to hear Boyd's explanation, but she didn't think Lieutenant Easterling would be crazy about the idea.

"Thanks for sticking up for me," Nancy said as she and Dave drove back toward the college.

"Just because he's a cop doesn't mean he's got a right to be rude," Dave answered. "So what happens now? Do you quit the case?"

"Absolutely not! I know we're close to breaking this thing wide open. The more we learn, the closer we get. Let's go back to the fraternity to see if Maury has broken into that second diskette."

"Do you think Boyd's the killer?" Dave asked.

Nancy shrugged. "It's obvious that he has something to hide. But is he the murderer? It's still too early to tell."

Dave wanted to work out, so Nancy dropped him off at the gym before returning to the fraternity house. When she went upstairs to Maury's room, she was startled to find Diana DeMarco there, sitting next to him in front of his computer.

"What are you doing here?" Nancy asked the brunette.

"Oh, hi." Diana looked embarrassed. "I've been trying to find you, Nancy. You weren't in the dorm, so I tried here."

"Diana knows a lot about programming," Maury explained. "I asked her if she wanted to give me a hand." Suddenly he looked doubtful. "Is that okay?" He looked at Diana. "I mean, maybe you shouldn't be looking at this stuff . . ." His voice trailed off.

Nancy and Diana regarded each other. After a long silence Diana spoke up. "Look, I know you don't trust me, and you have no reason to. But after our talk, I realized I couldn't just run away. I really cared for Wayne, and I want to know who killed him and why."

"What about your job with Subliminal Suggestions?" Nancy asked.

"I—I don't know. I haven't really given them anything about Edberg's study yet," Diana said. "Being with Wayne made me question the ethics of spying. I haven't decided yet." She straightened in her chair. "But after what Maury and I have seen on these diskettes, I know I have to stay here until this mystery is solved."

"Why?" asked Nancy, hurrying over to the computer. "What have you found?"

"Well, I broke the code to get into the blocked diskette," Maury told her.

Nancy felt a rush of adrenaline. "And?"

"Professor Edberg's data seemed to prove that subliminal tapes worked really well," he explained. "But I had trouble following his interpretation of the evidence. Apparently Wayne had the same problem, so he reevaluated all the data. The second disk has Wayne's results. He worked through all the data, eliminated the statistical discrepancies, and when he was done—"

"What did he find?" Nancy asked.

"Wayne concluded that, while the study doesn't *disprove* the effects of subliminal suggestion, it doesn't *prove* it either. In each group some students improved, some stayed the same, and some even got worse."

Nancy thought about this for a moment. "So what you're saying is—"

Diana broke in. "What he's saying is that Wayne discovered that Edberg was lying! Edberg falsified the data to support the conclusions he and Boyd were looking for."

114

Chapter

Thirteen

FOR A LONG moment, Nancy just stared at Maury and Diana. "Wow," she said. "That certainly puts a new twist on things."

Her mind raced, trying to make sense of the case in light of this revelation. "If Edberg falsified his results and Wayne found out, Edberg's entire career and reputation would be destroyed. He might have seen killing Wayne as the only way to protect everything he'd built for himself."

"What about that Boyd guy?" Maury asked. "The one Dave recognized."

That was another possibility, Nancy realized. "Maybe Boyd and Wayne were trying to dupe Edberg. If Wayne was working for Positive Tapes, he could have been feeding Edberg the false data and keeping a correct record for his own purposes."

"So you think Boyd knew from the start that they wouldn't be able to prove that the tapes worked?" Diana asked.

"It's possible. He could have hired Wayne to make sure that Edberg would see student test results that seemed to confirm that they worked." Nancy's mind was working a mile a minute. "We know that Dave Webb saw Boyd near the psych building before Wayne was killed. The question is, what was he doing there? Maybe Wayne tried to blackmail Boyd. Maybe he threatened to tell Edberg, so Boyd decided to kill Wayne."

Diana shook her head adamantly. "That's not the Wayne I knew! He was outraged by dishonesty and fraud!"

"People sometimes aren't what they seem to be," Nancy responded. "But maybe you're right. After all, you knew Wayne. I didn't. The point is, we've got to find a way to determine whether Boyd or Edberg is our culprit. It might even turn out that they're in it together."

Diana frowned. "It doesn't sound like you have any hard evidence so far," she pointed out.

"There might be something that could help answer your questions in Parker's file," Maury suggested to Nancy. "Unfortunately, I *still* can't find the file."

"That's odd. Have you found the records for

all the other students in the study?" Nancy asked.

Maury nodded. "There was a master list of students who've participated. I've been able to find files on anyone I looked for—except Parker. At last I thought I'd finally found it." He tapped a few keys to bring Parker's file up on the computer screen. "This is what I got."

On the screen were the words *File deleted.*

Letting out a sigh of disappointment, Nancy said, "Someone erased Parker's file. This tells us something, at least. Someone had something to hide, so they deleted Parker's file. But now we'll never know what it was."

"Uh, Nancy, there's something I haven't told you." Diana looked sheepish. She reached into her purse, which was sitting on the floor, and pulled out a third computer disk. "This was in Wayne's computer. I had it in a different pocket from the others. I haven't looked at it yet."

Nancy felt a thrill of excitement as Maury took the disk from Diana.

"It's unlabeled," he remarked. He popped the disk into his computer, and his fingers danced over the keys. Letters and numbers flashed on the screen.

"It has a blocking sequence similar to the one on Wayne's other disk," Maury murmured. "Shouldn't be too hard to get into it now."

He tried several times as the two girls watched, and finally he said, "Voilà! 'Wright, Parker, test subject.' Am I the best, or what?"

Nancy leaned forward excitedly. There on the screen was Edberg's file on Parker. "So what are we looking for?" Maury asked Nancy.

Nancy thought for a few moments as Maury flipped through the file, bringing up page after page of records. "Is there a list of the music they had Parker listen to?" she asked.

"Yup! It's one of the variables they were testing. Did the kind of music have any effect on the ability of the listener to pick up the subliminal message, that sort of thing. Here's Parker's music list. Anything particular you have in mind?"

"Yes," Nancy said, looking over his shoulder. She pointed to a title that had appeared on the screen. "That's it!" Listed among the selections was Johnny Lightning's "Cosmic Mind Control." The date next to it indicated that the song was a new addition that Parker had started to listen to only a couple of weeks ago.

"Something strange happens to Parker when he hears that song," Nancy explained. "And I want to find out why. Ned and Bess are with Parker at the infirmary now. Maybe they've made some progress."

Nancy arrived at the campus infirmary soon after her meeting with Maury and Diana. She still had misgivings about bringing Diana into the investigation, but she had to admit that Diana had been helpful. She and Maury had done terrific work on the computer diskettes. Now, if only Dr. Cohen was as successful.

As Nancy entered Dr. Cohen's office, she saw that Ned was leaning against the wall, while Bess sat on a corner of the doctor's desk. Both of them gestured for Nancy to be quiet. Parker sat on a chair, looking edgy and nervous while Dr. Cohen sat near him, talking quietly.

"How's it going?" Nancy whispered to Ned, going over to him.

"They've just finished taking a break," Ned told her, speaking softly. "Dr. Cohen has established that Parker goes into a highly suggestible state as soon as he hears that Johnny Lightning tune."

Dr. Cohen glanced over at Nancy, flashing her a friendly smile. "We're just about to play the song again."

"I'm ready," Parker said, taking a deep breath.

The doctor reached over to his cassette player, which sat on the floor. He flicked it on, and the opening chords of "Cosmic Mind Control" boomed out. Johnny Lightning's raspy, compelling voice began to sing.

"No, I don't want to show it,
But darlin', you know it,
I feel weak when I try to be strong.
'Though I know what you're asking is wrong
wrong wrong wrong wrong
I just can't resist
your cosmic mind control!"

"Look at Parker!" Bess whispered to Nancy.

Parker's entire manner had transformed, Nancy saw. Now that he had fallen into a hypnotic trance, he looked relaxed and peaceful. His eyelids fluttered, and his eyes were only half open.

Dr. Cohen lowered the volume on the cassette player, but "Cosmic Mind Control" continued to play softly in the background. "Parker, how do you feel?" Dr. Cohen asked.

"I feel good," Parker answered dreamily. "Nice."

"Do you like the music?"

"Oh, yes, it's my favorite song."

"Do you remember this song making you feel good before?" Dr. Cohen asked in a steady, calm voice.

"Sure."

"Is there anything different now?"

"Your voice . . . is different. And . . . you're asking me questions. Usually the voice just tells me things."

Ned leaned toward Nancy. "He's talked about this voice all afternoon," he explained in a hushed whisper. "The doctor has been trying to get him to identify whose voice it is. So far no go."

"But that doesn't make any sense," Nancy said softly. "The message is supposed to be *subliminal*, which means the person doesn't hear anything but the music or ocean or whatever. They can't actually *hear* the message."

120

Ned looked at her, astonished. "You're right," he said in a low voice. "I hadn't even thought about that. We'll have to ask the doctor when he brings Parker out of the trance."

"What sort of things does the voice tell you, Parker?" the doctor was continuing.

"It tells me to obey. It says it's my friend."

"And do you do what it tells you to do?"

"I try. But sometimes . . ."

"Yes?" Dr. Cohen prompted.

Parker said nothing.

"Do you remember your last study session with Wayne, Parker?" Dr. Cohen asked, taking a new approach.

"Yes."

"Tell me all about that night," Dr. Cohen encouraged.

Parker leaned back in his chair, and a soft smile came over his face. He looked almost happy. "Wayne was mad at me, but then he cooled off. He said I really was a good test subject and a good student," Parker said dreamily. "But he thought this might be our last session."

"Why was that?"

"He said he thought the study was about to end."

"Did he say why?"

Parker shook his head. "No. I was in the chair, and then the music started."

"What music was playing?"

"I don't know. It had soft flutes and bells. . . ."

Nancy leaned over to Bess. "Like the tape Boyd played for us at Positive Tapes," she whispered.

"And then?" Dr. Cohen prompted Parker.

"Then the song came on—Johnny Lightning. Wayne is in the room with me . . . but he doesn't hear the music. He takes out a book. . . . He doesn't need to pay much attention while I'm listening to the tapes."

A note of anxiety crept into Parker's voice as his story shifted into present tense. Bess jumped off the desk and took a step toward Parker, but Dr. Cohen waved her off.

"He's upset," Bess protested.

"We've got to let him live through it," the doctor said urgently.

Parker was babbling now. "The voice . . . the voice is talking to me. Wayne has his back to me, he's just reading. The voice tells me to reach into my pocket. . . ."

Nancy exchanged a wide-eyed look with Ned, and she knew they were thinking the same thing. This was amazing!

"My gun, the one my father gave me, is in my hand!" Parker went on, becoming more and more agitated. "I don't remember taking it from my desk at home, but I remember the voice told me to get a gun."

Wild-eyed, Parker leapt to his feet. He jerked his head around, as though he were seeing the lab instead of his actual surroundings. Now he was reacting as if the mysterious voice were speaking directly to him.

"No! I don't want to shoot him! Wayne turns around. He sees the gun in my hand. He puts his hands up and says, 'Please, Parker, don't!' The voice is still ordering me! No, no, please, no! I can't shoot him! Don't make me! No!"

Nancy took a step toward Parker. "You've got to bring him out of it, Doctor," she implored. "He's going to injure himself!"

Parker flailed his arms. In the next instant his whole body jerked, as though he himself had been shot. Then he collapsed to the floor.

Chapter

Fourteen

P ARKER!" Nancy cried, rushing toward the inert figure. She and Bess reached him at the same time.

Dr. Cohen immediately switched off the music, a look of concern etching his features. A moment later Parker opened his eyes, blinked a few times, and looked around.

"Are you okay?" Bess asked.

As the others crowded around, Parker sat up shakily and shook his head. "What happened? What am I doing on the floor?"

Dr. Cohen helped Parker up and into a chair. "You just reexperienced the murder," he explained.

Parker turned pale. "Did—did I kill Wayne?"

"We still don't know, pal," Ned said, resting a

reassuring hand on Parker's shoulder. "You were seeing something that really freaked you out, and you collapsed before you could tell us exactly what happened."

A steely glint of determination lit Parker's green eyes. "I want to try again," he said firmly.

Nancy could see that Parker was still very shaken. As much as she wanted to get at the truth, she worried about his mental state. "We can wait a while, Parker," she said. "This is obviously very hard on you."

Parker jumped up and pounded a balled fist into the open palm of his other hand. "I don't care about that!" he cried. "This is important. I have to know—I have to!"

"Hey, take it easy. It'll be okay," Bess reassured Parker, hugging him. She looked from Nancy to Ned to Dr. Cohen. "This is tearing him apart," she said. "The sooner he can learn the truth, the better."

"I agree," the doctor said. "But let's give him a few minutes to rest."

Nancy decided not to mention her thoughts about Parker actually hearing a voice. The explanation might become clear as Parker relived his experience.

Parker stood up and began doing stretching exercises. Soon his breathing was back to normal, and he was noticeably more relaxed. At last he nodded to the doctor and sat back down. "I'm ready to try again," he said.

Once more Johnny Lightning's voice rasped

through the room, and Parker immediately dropped into a hypnotic trance. Dr. Cohen spoke soothingly to Parker, bringing him quickly through the events of Thursday night, until they were back at the moment when Parker pulled the gun from his pocket.

This time the doctor was ready for Parker's distress, and he talked him through it, calming him. Now Parker was relaxed as he recalled what happened next. He leaned comfortably against the back of the chair. Nancy was surprised to note how natural he sounded.

"Parker, did you shoot Wayne?" Dr. Cohen asked.

"No. I couldn't. I pointed the gun at him, but I couldn't pull the trigger, even though the voice kept telling me to do it."

Nancy exchanged triumphant looks with Ned and Bess. Parker *hadn't* pulled the trigger!

"So what happened when you refused to kill Wayne?" Dr. Cohen asked next.

"He came out of his room."

" 'He'?"

Parker appeared not to have heard Dr. Cohen's question. "And then he and Wayne argued, and he took the gun away from me," Parker went on.

"Who is this 'he'?" Bess spoke up softly.

"And then he shot him!" Parker cried, leaping to his feet. "He pulled the trigger, and Wayne fell."

"Who, Parker? *Who* pulled the trigger?" Ned demanded, unable to restrain himself.

But Nancy knew. "You guys, think of who had a room to come out of in that lab?" she asked, her heart pounding with excitement. "Who was watching all the time, through the two-way mirror in the lab? Who had a microphone in that little room and knew how to use it to speak softly into Parker's ears through the headphones, while Parker sat listening to tapes? Who knew how to hypnotize him, had probably done it over and over again until he knew that Parker was under his complete control?"

Her friends and Dr. Cohen were looking at her as if she had lost her mind, but Nancy couldn't stop her line of reasoning.

"Who knew Parker so well that he felt certain he could order him to commit murder and be obeyed?" she said. "Who else, but Dr. Edberg!"

Suddenly Parker was no longer in his trance. He was wide awake and in complete control. "Nancy is right," he said calmly. "It *was* Edberg!"

"How do you feel, Parker?" Dr. Cohen asked later that afternoon.

"Like I just finished competing in the Nationals," Parker answered. "I feel emotionally and physically drained. But I feel relieved, too. I know I'm not a murderer."

For the last several hours, Parker had recalled everything Dr. Edberg had ordered him to do Thursday night in the psychology lab. Then, when Parker was ready, Dr. Cohen hypnotized him one last time and cancelled out any posthypnotic suggestions Edberg had given him.

"You see," the doctor explained to Ned, Nancy, and Bess, "that's how Edberg got Parker to take the gun. A posthypnotic suggestion is a command lodged in the subject's subconscious mind. So Parker was unaware of pocketing the gun, and he probably carried it around in his coat pocket for several days without recognizing that it was there."

"That's amazing!" Bess exclaimed. "Wouldn't he have felt it when he put his hands in his pockets?"

"Sure," Dr. Cohen replied. "But his conscious mind had been commanded not to register it as a gun."

"Edberg must have come back to the lab while Wayne was looking for me Thursday night," Parker said. "Wayne never checked the control room. He had set everything up for me beforehand, and when I put on the headphones, he just flipped the play switch on the alternate control panel in the lab."

Nancy recalled seeing the small panel of controls in the lab room. "But Edberg must have been listening to your tape on his own headphones in the control room," she added. "When he heard Johnny Lightning come on, he knew you'd fall into a trance, and he began to talk to you."

"And of course he was able to watch everything through the mirror," Ned put in.

Parker stood up and started pacing back and forth in front of Dr. Cohen's desk, too excited to sit still any longer. "I remember now," he said, raking a hand through his red hair. "Edberg had been hypnotizing me for a couple of weeks. Wayne was usually in the lab with me, while Edberg was in the control room. So Wayne didn't know that Edberg was actually talking to me through the headphones—he must have assumed that Edberg was just observing me through the one-way glass. Edberg talked to me only during that one song. Since I didn't know if I was one of the participants hearing the subliminal tape or not, I assumed that Edberg's talking to me was another part of the experiment. Now I realize he was getting me used to being hypnotized."

"You're right," Dr. Cohen said. "Finally, the song alone was enough to put you under." The doctor sat with his elbows on his desk, the fingers of both hands entwined, with his chin resting on his thumbs. "But how did he know to choose you instead of one of the other students?"

"I think I remember now," Parker responded. He stopped pacing. "Early in the study I had an interview alone with Edberg. During part of it he told me to watch his finger, and he moved it slowly in front of my eyes while he talked and talked. I felt dizzy, and later I glanced at his notes. He'd written, 'highly suggestible.' So I guess he knew I was easy to hypnotize."

Nancy and Ned sat together on the couch,

holding hands. Now Nancy spoke. "The rest is easy. Edberg was going to use Parker to kill Wayne." She turned her attention to Parker. "He knew you had a grudge against Wayne, and he knew you had a temper. He just assumed you'd be willing to kill him. But when you resisted, Edberg had to come out and do it himself. He must have been wearing gloves, so only your prints were on the gun, Parker."

"That's right. He told me to forget everything. Then he ran out of the room—and the next thing I knew, I was outside, stumbling into the snow."

Ned let out a low whistle. "He was probably still in the building when we found the body!" he exclaimed. "Then he slipped out before the police arrived."

"There are still some things I don't get," Bess said. "First, there's Edberg's alibi. Did his wife lie for him?"

"That's the most obvious explanation," Nancy agreed, "but it may not be the right one. We'll just have to find out when we catch Edberg."

Bess crinkled up her nose. "The other thing is—well, why? Why did Professor Edberg want to kill his research assistant?"

Nancy told the others what Maury and Diana had discovered on Wayne Perkins's computer disks. "We knew the results of the study had been falsified, but the one thing we couldn't figure out was *who* had done it. It must have been Edberg. Something must have made Wayne suspicious enough to copy Edberg's records and then reanalyze them. That's how he learned that Edberg had doctored the results," she concluded.

Bess still didn't look convinced. "But why was he lying? I mean, wouldn't that put his whole career in jeopardy?"

"I bet that's where Larry Boyd fits in," Nancy said. "We still need to find out why he was on campus that night. But I'll bet it has something to do with all those government contracts Boyd kept talking about. There's a lot of money at stake here. Edberg himself told us that whoever can prove that these tapes really work stands to make huge profits. Maybe he convinced Edberg to falsify the study's results."

Bess's face lit up with understanding. "If Diana's right about how honorable Wayne was, he must have threatened to expose Dr. Edberg's fraud. Maybe Edberg tried to bribe Wayne and was rebuffed. So Edberg had only one choice left."

"Murder!" Parker said.

A moment of silence filled the office as they all considered the story they had pieced together. Then Ned spoke up. "So now what do we do?" He turned to Nancy. "From what you've told me about Easterling, he's never going to buy this story."

"It *is* pretty farfetched," Dr. Cohen agreed. "And we've just destroyed some of the proof. Parker isn't hypnotized anymore, so we can't demonstrate the effect of the song on him."

"We've got a problem here," Nancy agreed.

"We have no hard and fast evidence, and it's a very tangled case. Lieutenant Easterling is not going to be a friendly audience, that's for sure." She sighed. "We've still got some heavy-duty thinking to do, guys."

Glancing at the clock, Nancy saw that it was already late afternoon. "Is anybody else hungry?" she asked. "I say we figure out what to do over a pizza."

"Nan, could you pass me a slice with pepperoni?" Ned asked.

He, Nancy, Bess, and Parker were sitting together in Lorenzo's, a popular student hangout near the Emerson campus. None of them had eaten since that morning, and only a few slices were left of the two large pizzas they had ordered.

"So what do we do?" Parker wondered aloud, as he finished his third slice of sausage and mushroom pizza. He turned to Nancy. "Are you really going to go to the police like you promised Dr. Cohen?" he asked.

Dr. Cohen had declined their invitation to join them. As they'd left his office he had tried to persuade them to go to the police, or at least to Captain Backman. They had promised to do that first thing in the morning. In turn, he had promised to wait until morning to contact the authorities himself.

"I don't see how we can avoid it," Nancy said, answering Parker's question. "We've got to bring Easterling into the case."

"But you said yourself that he'll never believe us," Bess protested. She took a sip of soda, then crunched down on some small ice cubes.

"That's right," Nancy said. "The only way he'll believe us is if he hears Professor Edberg himself make a confession." She paused for effect and then said, "And I have a plan that will get the professor to do just that!"

Chapter
Fifteen

That's right, Professor Edberg, midnight tonight, in the psych lab." Nancy paused while Professor Edberg said something. "Yes, that will be fine." Nancy hung up the pay phone in the back of Lorenzo's and turned to Ned, Bess, and Parker, who were clustered around her. "He bought it," she told them.

"This could be very dangerous, Nan," Bess said, biting her lip. "Edberg could be capable of anything."

Nancy looped one arm each around Ned and Parker's shoulders and gave them both a quick squeeze. "That's why I'm taking these two heroes along as backup," she said.

Ned ducked his head like a cowboy hero from

an old movie and said, "Aw, shucks, ma'am, ah appreciate the confidence y'all have in me an' mah pardner."

They all laughed nervously. Nancy knew that Bess was right. Her plan was a risky one. They just had to hope that it would work.

When she'd called Edberg, she'd told him who she was and said that she had important information about Wayne's death. This information was very sensitive, she'd said. She only felt safe sharing it with him face-to-face. Now that he'd agreed to meet her, the plan was in motion.

Glancing at her watch, she saw that it was six P.M. That gave them plenty of time to prepare for their rendezvous.

Five hours later, Nancy carefully picked the lock to the back door of the psychology building. She entered cautiously, followed by Ned and Parker. They tiptoed through the building and up the stairs to the second-floor lab where Wayne had been killed. They slipped under the criss-crossed police tape in front of the door.

"You guys had better get ready in the observation booth," Nancy said, nodding toward the door next to the mirrored wall.

"What's the hurry?" Parker asked. "Edberg's not going to be here for another hour."

Nancy shook her head. "I wouldn't count on him waiting that long. I know he's going to arrive early. He thinks I can't get into the building without him unlocking the door. He told me he'd leave the front door open. He'll be here within twenty minutes—I guarantee it."

While the boys entered the observation booth, closing the door behind them, Nancy examined her surroundings. She shivered when she saw the big reddish brown stain on the carpet next to the black leather recliner. Stepping carefully around it, she walked over to the control panel against the wall. She played with a few switches, checking everything out. From what Parker had said, these duplicated some of the controls on the more complex control panel inside the observation booth.

Edberg had taken a chance when he assumed that Wayne would start the tape from out there instead of entering the booth. But then, Nancy thought, he must have known Wayne's habits.

Nancy flicked on the microphone built into the control panel. "Can you guys hear me?" she asked.

"Loud and clear, Nan." Ned's voice boomed out from the two stereo speakers mounted high up in the corners on either side of the mirrored wall.

"How's the recording equipment working?" she asked.

There was no answer for a moment, and she worried that there was a problem. Then the speakers crackled, and her own voice came over them, saying, "How's the recording equipment working?"

"Very cute, guys," she muttered. "Okay— quiet on your end from now on, got it?"

While she waited for Professor Edberg, Nancy sat in the recliner, thinking over their plan. She glanced at her watch. It was almost eleven-thirty. She hoped Bess was taking care of her part of the plan. Dr. Edberg should be here right about—

"Well, Miss Drew, I certainly did not expect you to arrive before me. Perhaps you would be so kind as to explain how you got into a locked building, as well as your cryptic remarks over the telephone this evening."

With a sudden gasp, Nancy leapt out of the recliner. Professor Edberg was standing in the doorway of the lab.

Tonight the professor was dressed casually, in jeans, boots, and a bulky blue parka. A knit cap was pulled down over his ears. Glimpsing the menacing look in his eyes, Nancy hoped that she'd been right to take the risk of confronting him.

"How I got into the building is unimportant, Dr. Edberg," Nancy said, trying to sound more confident than she felt. "I'm sure you are much more interested in my purpose in meeting you."

The professor closed the door behind him and took several steps toward her. "You said you had information about Wayne's death."

"That's right, I do—information that concerns you directly. You see, I've discovered who killed him."

Edberg laughed. "Come now, my dear, that's

old news. If you've brought me out this late just to rehash this dreadful case, I'm going to be quite angry." He turned to go. "I've already told you how sorry I am for your friend Parker Wright, but after all, he has only himself to blame."

"Parker isn't the killer, and you know it!" Nancy said sharply.

Edberg turned on his heel. "Oh?" he said, a hard edge creeping into his voice. He took a step closer to her. "Since you're such a clever detective, suppose you tell me what it is you think I know."

Nancy gave a matter-of-fact shrug. "You killed Wayne when he discovered that you were falsifying the results of your study," she told him.

Edberg's change of expression was terrifying. His face turned a blazing crimson and became contorted with rage. His dark beard bristled. "Why, you—" he growled, as his fists clenched.

Nancy held up her hands. "Hey, take it easy!" she said. "I'm not trying to get you into trouble. I know what's at stake here, and I don't blame you. Besides"—she dropped her voice to a confidential whisper—"Parker Wright doesn't mean much to me anyway. After all, I just met him on Thursday. I could forget what I know—if someone made it worth my while."

"What about the rest of your friends?" Dr. Edberg asked, arching a brow. "That blond girl who was with you the other day? And your boyfriend?"

Nancy gave a dismissive wave of her hand.

"They're so naive. I haven't told them anything. This is between you and me. Let them think this is one case that beat me! I only have a couple of questions."

Edberg shot her an icy smile. "I could see right away that you're a bright girl, Nancy," he said. "Perhaps we should both drop our guard and play straight with each other. Now, what is it you want to ask me?"

"Well, I know how much this project is worth. Is Boyd paying you to falsify data? Or were you just going to take a percentage of the government contracts?"

After a long hesitation, the professor replied, "Both."

"Boyd was in on Wayne's murder, then?" Nancy pressed.

"No, of course not!"

"Then what was he doing on campus Thursday night? Dave Webb saw him."

Edberg shrugged. "He just stopped by to give me my monthly payoff. After Dave and I separated, I drove out of the parking lot, then came back to the psych building to meet Boyd. I took the money, and then he left. I never mentioned Wayne to him—I'm sure he has no idea I killed him."

Nancy tried not to show her triumph. She had actually gotten Edberg to admit to the murder! She could see that he considered himself very clever. He was actually enjoying telling her about his criminal activities.

"So you didn't return home, as you told the police," Nancy said. "How did you get your wife to lie for you?" she asked.

Professor Edberg laughed. "Actually, it was quite simple. She didn't know she was lying! I've been hypnotizing her for years. A word or two whispered in her ear, and she really believed I was home, taking a shower, at the very time poor Wayne was being shot."

Nancy took a deep breath before asking her next question. "Why did you need to kill Wayne?"

"Good question," he said, smiling at her as if she were one of his students. "Wayne really was a wonderful assistant. If only he'd been willing to go along. But his foolish ethics wouldn't permit it. You see, it's really his own fault that he's dead."

Edberg gave Nancy a shifty, confidential look. "Wayne came to me more than a week ago. I had been watching him, of course, and knew that his suspicions had started much earlier. He said he thought I'd made some honest mistakes, and he wanted to warn me that my research was flawed. Such a good student, worrying about his old professor! That's when I took him into my confidence. I told him about the bribes Boyd was paying me to alter the results of the study and said that he could get his share, too."

Nancy didn't like the evil glint that had come into the professor's eyes as he spoke. But she felt that as long as she kept him talking, he probably wouldn't do anything to harm her. "Why didn't Wayne turn you in as soon as he knew about the fraud?" she asked.

"He liked me too much," Dr. Edberg said with an amused laugh. "He thought he could convince me to turn my back on millions of dollars! That's what my share will be worth when Positive Tapes gets those fat government contracts."

He shook his head sadly. "But things could never be the same between Wayne and me. The tension those last few days was dreadful. On Wednesday he told me he was going to blow the whistle and bring me up on academic charges to the faculty ethics committee. The fool thought I would just sit back and let him ruin my entire career! I knew what I had to do, and it all went perfectly—until that weakling, Wright, refused to pull the trigger."

"I wondered about that," Nancy said. "I mean, that hypnosis trick was really smart, but why did you have to use Parker?"

Dr. Edberg shrugged. "Once Wayne expressed his initial doubts, I thought *I* might eventually have to kill Wayne. I needed someone for a patsy, and Parker was the natural choice." He paused thoughtfully before going on. "It was such a good plan. I waited in the observation room. I knew Parker was primed and ready—I'd been hypnotizing him for days."

"But I thought he met with you only once a week," Nancy cut in, shooting Edberg a puzzled glance.

"That's all he remembered," Edberg said, a sly smile on his face. "Actually he was here every day last week, as well as the week before."

Nancy nodded her understanding. "But you gave him posthypnotic commands not to remember those sessions." She couldn't believe how twisted Edberg was. He'd manipulated everyone around him without any concern for what it might do to them.

"Exactly!" the professor replied proudly. "I even gave him false memories to account for the lost time."

A dark frown came over his face as he added, "But then Parker balked at shooting Wayne—which I should have anticipated, of course. As you may know, a person who has been hypnotized is merely in an altered state of consciousness and won't do anything under hypnosis that is against his or her ethics or beliefs. However, I was counting on the fact that the hostility between Parker and Wayne was so great that Parker would be willing to kill Wayne. He was not. Imagine my frustration—I had to come out, grab the gun away from him, and shoot Wayne myself! Still, it all worked out."

Nancy faced the professor squarely. "Except for me," she said.

"Except for you," he agreed. "Now, what am I going to do about you?"

"Why don't you cut me in on some of the money?" Nancy suggested.

"Oh, no," Edberg said, shaking his head.

"That won't work. It's blackmail, you see, and I could never trust you to keep quiet. You're too willing to sell out Parker, who is supposed to be your friend. You wouldn't hesitate to turn me over once you had your money. No, Nancy, I'm afraid there's only one thing I can do about you."

His right hand dipped into his jacket pocket and immediately reappeared, clutching a small automatic pistol.

Professor Edberg pointed the pistol at Nancy, an evil smile on his face. "Say goodbye, Nancy Drew."

Chapter
Sixteen

A FEELING of dread welled up in Nancy as she stared at the pistol.

"Wait!" she exclaimed. "Before you shoot me, there's one more thing I need to tell you!" She knew she would have to talk fast if she wanted to stay alive.

Edberg's eyes narrowed. "These are going to be among your very last words—choose them wisely."

"How are you going to explain *this* murder?" she challenged.

"There won't be anything to explain," the professor said, waving the gun in the air. "No one knows you came here. My car is just outside. We'll take a nice little drive out of town. After I shoot you, I'll dump your body in the woods. No doubt someone will report you missing, but no one will even find your body until the spring thaw. Now, what is it you have to tell me?"

Nancy took a deep breath. "Just that it's all over—give yourself up!"

Edberg guffawed with laughter. "Oh, come now, Miss Drew! You can do better than that!"

"You don't believe me?"

"Of course not!" he scoffed.

"Okay, then—" She hoped this would work. "Hit it, guys!" she cried out.

A loud staccato crackle rippled out from the two loudspeakers on the walls. Startled, Edberg jerked his head toward the noise. Then the professor's voice boomed out: "I had to come out, grab the gun away from him, and shoot Wayne myself."

Edberg gaped at Nancy, his face purple with rage. "What have you done? Who's in there?" he demanded, looking at the two-way mirror.

"That's your confession, Professor!" Nancy told him. "Every word recorded on your own equipment, in your own lab."

"You little fool! Do you think you can get away with this?" he asked, raising his voice. "You're all fools. There's no way out of that observation booth except through here. I'll kill you all. Now, come out of there!"

When no one emerged from the control room, he said, "All right then, I'm coming in." Edberg gestured at Nancy with his gun. "Move." Reaching out with his free hand, he grabbed her shoulder, spun her around to face the door, and gave her a shove.

Nancy was surprised at how strong he was. She stumbled toward the door to the observation booth.

"Open it!" Edberg ordered.

Nancy took a deep breath. Ned was resourceful, she told herself. He'd think of something. She opened the door.

The observation room was dark, she saw. She couldn't see the guys, but she was acutely aware that Edberg was right behind her, his gun poking her in the small of the back. He gave her another shove and ordered, "Step in and turn on the light."

Nancy flicked on the light in the little room. Edberg pushed her in, following close behind her. He blinked in surprise, and Nancy took two steps back and spun around to face him.

Except for Nancy and Edberg, the room was empty. The guys weren't there! The tape of Edberg's confession continued to play.

"What's going on?" Dr. Edberg demanded.

Nancy was wondering the same thing. Before she could say anything, a voice spoke from *above* them.

"Peekaboo!"

Startled, Edberg looked up. The voice was coming from a wall speaker. Suddenly the chair at the console was propelled across the room, and the professor jumped out of the way. Nancy saw Parker scrunched under the console table, microphone in hand.

Nancy didn't waste a second. As Parker leapt out from under the console, Nancy lashed out with a terrific karate kick, sending the gun flying from Dr. Edberg's hand. At the same moment, Ned jumped out from behind the door. He and Parker pounced on Edberg like a pair of panthers.

The three of them went to the floor in a struggling mass. For a moment it seemed that Ned and Parker would overpower Edberg, but the professor managed to throw them both off.

He lurched to his feet, his eyes searching the floor for his gun, but it had skidded under the control console when Nancy kicked it out of his hand. Nancy grabbed his arm, trying to restrain him with a judo hold, but he flicked her away. Before any of the teens could react, Edberg reeled toward the door.

"Stop him! He's getting away!" Nancy cried.

Edberg burst out of the observation booth with Nancy, Ned, and Parker hot on his heels. He ran to the door of the lab, threw it open—and crashed into Marcus Backman.

Edberg threw a wild punch at Backman. Captain Backman caught Edberg's hand in midpunch. Spinning Edberg around, Backman wrapped his muscular arms around the profes-

sor. A moment later he was snapping handcuffs
around Edberg's wrists.

"Don't run out on us, Professor," Backman
rumbled. "We've got lots to talk about."

Behind Backman stood Bess and Dr. Cohen.
Ned and Parker had raced out of the control booth after Nancy, and Bess shot them a
wide-eyed look. "Are we on time?" she asked.
"We had a little trouble locating Captain Backman."

"You did fine, Bess," Nancy assured her with a
grin. "Your timing couldn't be more perfect."

"Now," Marcus Backman said, looking at
Nancy, Ned, and Parker, "Bess tells me you were
going to get the professor's confession on tape.
How about playing it for me?"

"Well, Nan, I think you've set a personal
record for the biggest investigative team you've
ever put together for a case," Ned joked early the
next morning.

He, Nancy, Parker, and Bess were standing on
the steps of the Emersonville police station with
Dr. Cohen and Captain Backman. Diana
DeMarco, Maury Becker, and Dave Webb were
also with them. The three of them had been
awakened by Nancy and her friends so that they
could help explain the case.

The group had been at the station for most of
the night. Soon after Dr. Edberg had been arrested, Captain Backman had called Lieutenant

Easterling and convinced him to meet the others and listen to the confession Ned and Parker had taped.

Easterling had listened to the tape three times. Then he'd gone to the interrogation room where Edberg was being held. When he came back, his attitude had changed from doubtful to apologetic.

"Edberg waived his right to a lawyer and confessed to everything," the lieutenant said, shaking his head. "Despite all the bragging he does on that tape you made, he's a pretty unstable individual. All the fight's gone out of him now."

"What about Larry Boyd?" Nancy asked.

"Oh, we've got lots to charge him with. Bribery, conspiracy. . . . I've sent a patrol car out to pick him up. It's a shame. You know, I've even used a couple of his tapes—the 'Stop Smoking' series." He paused to light a cigar. "Anyway, I guess I owe you an apology, Miss Drew. I didn't take you seriously. My mistake."

"That's okay," Nancy told him.

Turning to Parker, Easterling added, "I just assumed that you were guilty, kid. Guess I owe you an apology, too." They shook hands.

For the next couple of hours, Easterling questioned them all, separately and together, trying to follow the path of Nancy's investigation. Maury had brought along Wayne's computer diskettes, and the police took them as evidence.

At last Easterling had told them they were all free to go.

Now Nancy yawned. She glanced at her watch. "Wow, it's six in the morning!"

"I've got to get back to the campus security office," Captain Backman said in his deep voice. He shook Nancy's hand. "It was a pleasure working with you, Nancy." Turning to Dr. Cohen, he said, "Give you a ride back to campus, Paul?"

The two of them drove off. Maury and Dave headed for Dave's car, then paused to offer Diana a ride.

"Sure," she said. "But first I'd like a minute to talk with Nancy."

The two girls moved a few feet away from the others. "Thanks for convincing me to stay," Diana began. "I don't think I could have lived with myself if I'd run out without finding out who really killed Wayne. In my heart I knew Parker wasn't the real murderer."

"So what will you do now?" Nancy asked.

Diana shrugged. "I promised Lieutenant Easterling that I'd come back to town for the trial." She took a breath before adding, "But right now I'm going back to Pittsburgh to quit working for Subliminal Suggestions. I'm not cut out to be a spy. After coming here . . . well, I discovered that I like being a student again. Maybe I'll come back to Emerson and get a graduate degree."

"That sounds great! In psychology?"

"Absolutely!" The two girls laughed. Nancy and Diana gave each other a quick hug, then Diana left with Dave and Maury.

As Nancy stepped back over to Ned, Bess, and Parker, Parker turned to her with a sheepish expression. "Nancy, I don't know how I can ever thank you."

Nancy put a finger to her lips. "Shh. There's no need for thanks. You're Ned's friend—that makes you family."

Parker smiled at Nancy, then impulsively gave her a big hug.

"Hey, that's *my* girlfriend!" Ned joked. "You don't have to be *that* grateful."

Nancy and Parker broke off the embrace. Grinning at Ned, Nancy suggested, "How about breakfast?"

"Sounds great," Ned agreed. "Gus's Diner should just be opening up."

The four of them walked toward Nancy's blue Mustang, which was parked in the police lot. Bess and Parker walked arm in arm, smiling happily at each other. Bess wrapped both arms around Parker's waist and gave him a squeeze. "This was some way to get to know each other," she joked.

He paused to look into her eyes. "Actually, I'd like to get to know you a lot better, Bess," he said softly. Turning to Nancy and Ned, he added, "There's always spring break. Maybe the four of us could go somewhere together."

"That would be terrific," Nancy agreed. "And wherever we go, we'll make sure that there are no mysteries to solve there!"

"That's a nice wish," Ned whispered in her ear, "but I wouldn't count on it."

Nancy's next case:

Andy Devereux invites Nancy, Ned, and Bess to a sailing regatta near his family's estate in Annapolis, Maryland. Andy is the co-owner of a boat-designing company, and he all but guarantees that his boat will win the cup. But his hopes—and his life—are suddenly blown off course when the police arrest him for murder!

Andy's partner, Nick Lazlo, has vanished at sea, his boat stained with blood and riddled with bullet holes. Nancy's investigation into the company reveals that the business had a strange and unsavory side—both personally and financially. In a case of missing money, missing boats, and missing bodies, the most dangerous discovery of all may be the truth . . . in *MAKING WAVES*, Case #81 in the Nancy Drew Files™.